NO ONE HAS SOLVED THIS MYSTERY IN FIVE CENTURIES

Was King Richard III responsible for the smothering of his nephews, the little Princes in the Tower of London? Now, a modern day murderer stalks a quiet college town, claiming victims in the same way. When the beautiful chairman of the English department dies, John Forest, a young history professor beset by personal and romantic problems, must grapple with both mysteries. Then he learns he may be next on the killer's list. . . .

"Now is the winter of our discontent made glorious summer by *TO PROVE A VILLAIN.* For those bored or repelled by improbable macho detectives being churned out like inferior tasteless butter, *TO PROVE A VILLAIN* is dessert—refreshingly high entertainment told with warm wit. It's a compellingly one-sitting book, deftly crafted and well-characterized, with fair clues. If books were restaurants, it would get four stars."

—Jane Gottschalk, University of Wisconsin; mystery critic, scholar, and author

To Prove
A Villain

Guy M. Townsend

To Prove
A Villain

A mystery from **Perseverance Press**
Menlo Park, California

Art Direction and Design by Gary Page and Merit Media.
Additional Design by Richard Waldron.
Photography by Dean Fidelman.
Typography from disk by Accent Graphics.

Published by
  Perseverance Press
  P. O. Box 384
  Menlo Park, California 94026

Manufactured in the United States of America.

1 2 3—87 86 85

Library of Congress Catalog Card Number: 84–63065

ISBN: 0–9602676–2–X

To Joe for encouraging me
and to Jeanne for putting up with me

To Prove
A Villain

Part 1
Puzzle

1

first heard about it a little before nine o'clock Wednesday morning, by which time she had been dead for more than eight hours. Walking past the department chairman's office, I heard Miss Daggett's shrill, spinsterish voice saying:

"—ever asked to be murdered, it was that woman! There aren't many people in this world who will miss her."

I'm as curious as the next fellow, so I slowed my step and heard Marge Cominos say, in the patient voice that everyone in the history department marvelled at, "Really, Miss Daggett, I don't think you should say that about anyone. Dr. James-Tyrell had her faults, just like everyone else, but she had her good points, too."

I was right at the office door, and the name stopped me cold. "What's this?" I demanded. "What's this about Dr. James-Tyrell?"

Marian James-Tyrell was a highly competent scholar and teacher with an eye-catching face and figure. She was in her early to mid-thirties, about my age. After, some years before, surrendering my illusions that I was going to live forever, I had become acutely conscious of my own mortality, and deaths among my chronological peers never failed to shake me. They were forceful reminders that it was only a matter of time until my own number came up. I hadn't particularly liked Marian, but, besides being of an age with me, she was a colleague, and I was stunned by the news of her death.

Miss Daggett did not deign to reply to my brusque question. She just crossed her arms and settled prissily back in her swivel chair, her face wrapped in that smug look that some old people get when they hear they've outlived yet another fellow human.

Marge, who had been standing with her back to the door, spun around at my outburst.

"Oh!" she exclaimed. "Good morning, Dr. Forest. You haven't heard? Dr. James-Tyrell was killed in her home last night. The police are swarming all over the campus, asking questions of everyone. You just missed a detective who was here to see Dr. Hall. I suppose they'll get around to all of us before it's over."

Although, as far as I knew, Marge hadn't known Marian very well, she was clearly upset. Marge's problem was that she was just too damned nice. Come to think of it, though, she needed all the niceness she could muster for her job. She had been hired three years before as an unsubtle hint that Miss Daggett could retire without causing the department to fall to pieces, but Miss Daggett simply didn't take hints that she didn't like. As a result, the history department had possessed two full-time secretaries ever since, a fact which members of other departments were inclined to envy only if they had never met Miss Daggett.

I said to Marge, "What do you mean, 'killed'? Miss Daggett said something about murder."

"I really don't know, Dr. Forest. A friend of mine who works in the math department phoned just a minute ago and said that a policeman had told her that Dr. James would not be teaching his classes today and that they should all be cancelled. She got the impression that Dr. James was down at the police station."

Miss Daggett snorted and muttered something to the effect that he ought to be given a medal. I decided to ignore her. Of course, I'd been trying to ignore her for years without much success. Still, there wasn't much else to do but try. She could have been forced into retirement, but she was the daughter of Brookleigh's first president, and those in a position to force her out kept hoping that voluntary retirement on Miss Daggett's part would render such an unpleasant course of action unnecessary. In my opinion, which was shared by most people who knew her, that was one hundred percent wishful thinking.

4

Sarah Daggett wouldn't leave until she was dragged away by brute force, and even then she would fight all the way.

I asked a few more questions, but, aside from the fact—make that the rumor—that Marian had been smothered to death in her bed, Marge didn't have much more to tell.

I finally left her there with the old dragon and walked on down the dim corridor toward my office, noticing for the hundredth time the worn boards on the floor and the paint that was peeling from the walls between daunting, dusty portraits of dour and presumably long-dead politicians and businessmen who had once done something for, or to, Brookleigh College. It is an unwritten rule in American colleges today that the history department be housed in the oldest, most disreputable building on campus. A charitable explanation might be that it hones a historian's professional sensibilities to spend many hours a week in an environment unsullied by such modern conveniences as efficient heating and properly functioning toilet facilities. In fact, however, the history department gets treated like a poor and not quite respectable relative mainly because it lacks the clout and pizazz of the more new-fangled disciplines. People don't care much for history nowadays; all the smart money is on science and business.

I unlocked my office door, flipped on the overhead light, and deposited my briefcase in a ragged stuffed armchair before walking a few steps further down the hall to Roger Wyndham's office. I stopped in the doorway and said, " 'Lo, Rog. What have you heard about Marian James-Tyrell's death?"

All that was visible of him were the worn soles of the size-thirteen shoes he had propped up on his desk and the fingers on either side of the newspaper he was reading. At the sound of my voice he lowered his feet to the floor and tossed the newspaper aside, revealing a bearded face that always reminded me of a lecherous puppy. His eyes looked huge through the thick lenses of his heavy, horn-rimmed glasses.

"Damn all, John," he said, waving me to a straight-backed chair beside the door. "I was just looking through the paper, but there's nothing about it."

I told him what little I had gotten out of Marge, but he knew all that already. "Do you think Harrison killed her?" I asked.

"Damned if I know. If I were Harrison I'd have killed her long ago, but since he's put up with her for this long I don't see why he'd do it at this late date."

"What about for her money? She inherited the Tyrell Container Corporation fortune, didn't she?" Marian's father, Henry Tyrell, had founded the company and made it into a multi-million dollar operation before high blood pressure and a dicky heart brought his dynamic business career to a dead stop—literally—on the day before his sixty-seventh birthday. Roger, an American historian whose specialty was local history, knew far more about this than I did.

"Yeah, I know," he replied. "But Harrison already *had* access to the millions; he didn't have to kill Marian to get them."

He dug into the pocket of his shabby tweed coat and pulled out a nasty-looking pipe, which he proceeded to load from a humidor on his desk. As he was doing that he cocked his head to one side and looked at me with his grotesquely magnified eyes.

"You're not a local boy, are you, John?" he asked.

He knew that I wasn't, but I answered him anyway with a shake of my head.

"Then you may not know all there is to know about good old Marian. I, on the other hand, am a Brookleigh lad, born and bred, and I went to school with the luscious Tyrell lass. I had a terrible crush on her in high school, if the truth be told—along with half the school's male population."

"You seem to have gotten over it since then," I remarked. "At least, you're bearing up remarkably well under the loss."

"Puppy love, John. Mere puppy love." He dismissed it with a wave of his hand, depositing a dusting of tobacco crumbs atop the papers which littered his desk. "Marian was always a bit too high-powered for me. But at least I've always understood her, which is more than could be said for a lot of people, including old Henry." He replaced the lid on the humidor, then he negligently brushed his fingers on his jacket front to remove the tiny crumbs of tobacco which adhered to them. Roger was, not to put too fine a point on it, an unregenerate slob.

"Marian was always an enigma to her father," he continued. "Old Henry had started out poor, but he made his pile while Marian was still a little girl, and he always wanted her to take her place in society. When she finished high school, he sent her off to a posh women's college, expecting her to pick up a genteel baccalaureate and then come back home and live a life of cultured idleness.

"Marian, bless her stony little heart, had other ideas. In

6

college she became infected with a love for English literature, and, rather than come back to Brookleigh after receiving her B.A. and hang out around the country club until she latched onto some suitable mate, she proceeded to acquire a master's degree and a Ph.D. as well—and in near-record time."

He fell silent long enough to strike a large kitchen match and puff his pipe alight. Mercifully, he favored a decent-smelling mixture, rather than one of the blends that could have been patented by a manufacturer of fumigation supplies. He waved the match out with a flick of his wrist, tossed it into a large ash tray on his desk, and leaned back in his chair for a few contented puffs before he continued.

"She then continued to confound her father by taking a position as an English instructor at a large state university on the west coast. It was there that she met Harrison James, who was then a mathematics instructor on the same faculty. They were married soon after, and it was typical of Marian that she did not give up her own name but tacked it onto her new husband's with a hyphen."

He shook his head, saying, "I've never understood how that worked. I mean, whose name comes first, and why?"

"Nowadays," I responded, "it doesn't matter. People do it both ways and seem to be happy with it. It has always struck me as being a bit silly."

"Me, too," he agreed, "but Marian wouldn't have given a damn whether we thought it was silly or not. She did it because she wanted to do it, and that was that."

"How did she and Harrison get back here from the west coast?" I asked.

"Henry Tyrell died a short time after the two were married, leaving Marian's mother all alone, and Marian, worried that her mother might not be able to carry on by herself in the absence of her husband of some forty-odd years, inquired at the college here about openings for herself and Harrison. Both the English and the mathematics departments were fully staffed at the time, but the administration, mindful of the sizeable contributions Henry Tyrell had made to the college during his lifetime, and with an eye on possible future donations from his heir, managed to find places for both Marian and Harrison."

I raised an eyebrow at that, and Roger smiled crookedly. "I know, I know," he said. "And there were a good many people who felt the same way—including me. But it was soon evident that, however they had gotten their appointments, they were both fine additions to the faculty. Within a year or two Harrison had made something of a name for himself in some esoteric sub-branch of the mathematics field about which I have no knowledge and even less interest, and Marian, besides being an excellent scholar, turned out to be a dynamic teacher as well."

I interrupted. "Marian may have been good at her job—" Roger started to object, so I amended it. "Okay. Marian was good at her job, but she was a damned difficult woman to do business with. I butted heads with her more than once in faculty meetings, as you may recall."

"I recall, all right," Roger said with a grin, "but I'd be hard pressed to say which of you two was the most bull-headed."

I started to respond, but Roger plowed straight ahead.

"Like many other strong personalities," he said, cocking an eye at me, "Marian left most people either liking her a great deal or hating her just as much, and her arrogance and forceful manner caused those who hated her to considerably outnumber those who liked her. But her competence was unquestioned, John. You'll remember that when old Professor Burke resigned the chairmanship of the English department a couple of years back, Marian was one of only two members of the department who were seriously considered to fill the vacancy."

"All right," I said, conceding the point. Changing the subject slightly, I asked, "What happened to Marian's mother? I thought Marian and Harrison lived alone in the Tyrell mansion."

"They do," Roger said, "but when they first came back they lived in the carriage house on the estate. Ironically, Marian's mother died before Marian and Harrison finished their first year here, and they moved into the big house soon after."

"Marian was the sole heir, wasn't she?"

"Yes, and she inherited quite a bundle. But, you know," Roger added, as though thinking of it for the first time, "she and Harrison never let their considerable wealth affect their lives very much."

"The hell they didn't," I said. "How many college professors do you know who buy new Mercedes sedans and Porsche sports cars every year and spend every summer in Europe?"

"Not too many, I grant you," he replied. "But you've got to admit that, unlike a lot of other people with great wealth, they never acted as though they were better than the rest of us."

I thought about it for a moment and saw that he was right.

Half the faculty at Brookleigh had trouble making the mortgage payments and putting braces on their kids' teeth with the salaries they received, but neither Marian nor Harrison acted as though wealth had anything to do with a person's real worth. Whatever faults they might have had, flaunting their money was not one of them.

I took a different tack. "What about their marriage, Roger?"

"What about it?" he responded. "It was no worse than what passes for normal in our screwed-up age."

"You know what I mean, Roger. It's the worst-kept secret on campus that Marian was anything but a faithful wife."

Roger removed his glasses and ran his hand roughly down his face from his forehead to his chin. Without his glasses, his eyes looked quite normal. He put them on again before he spoke.

"Okay, John. So Marian like to fool around. But she has *always* fooled around, and Harrison has known about it all along. I can't say that I'd feel the same way, but Harrison appears to be—or to have been—a very understanding husband. In the end, Marian always tired of her extramarital flings, and their marriage continued along with scarcely a ripple on the surface. I wouldn't have called it a close marriage, but it was a damned sight better than a good many others I know about."

I wondered briefly if he was referring to my own late and unlamented marriage.

We lapsed into silence, each of us travelling down mental paths opened up by our conversation. My thoughts were about Harrison. Try as I would, I just couldn't see him in the role of a murderer. Then I smiled at the irony of that thought, because I *had* seen him in precisely that role on more than one occasion. Harrison's one interest outside of mathematics was the theater, and he had a major part in every play that the school's amateur theatrical society put on. Maybe he didn't have the talent to become a professional, but to my uneducated eye he was damned good. His performance of the title role in last year's production of *Richard III* was just about perfect.

For someone who knew him as a pleasant and attractive man, his hunch-backed appearance on stage in the opening scene was quite startling. The period costume and the padding on the shoulders did their part, but it was Harrison's acting ability that sent a shiver up my spine as he delivered Shakespeare's chilling lines:

Cheated of feature by dissembling nature,
Deform'd, unfinish'd, sent before my time
Into this breathing world, scarce half made up,
And that so lamely and unfashionable
That dogs bark at me as I halt by them;
Why, I, in this weak piping time of peace,
Have no delight to pass away the time,
Unless to spy my shadow in the sun
And descant on mine own deformity:
And therefore, since I cannot prove a lover,
To entertain these fair well-spoken days,
I am determined to prove a villain
And hate the idle pleasures of these days.

But however effective he was in acting the part, I just couldn't adjust my image of the real man to that of murderer. For one thing, except for the theater—in addition to his interest in acting, he also collected theatrical memorabilia, and one huge room in the Tyrell mansion was devoted to his collection—and mathematics, Harrison was an almost completely passionless man. Politics didn't bother him, not did the academic version thereof. He simply went along with whatever happened, as even-tempered as could be.

The ringing of the phone in my office disturbed my reverie. I said a hurried good-bye to Roger and went next door to answer it.

"Forest," I said, picking up the receiver as I walked around the desk to my chair.

"John? This is Ben Latta."

Latta was a friend and sometime student of mine. He was also a cop.

"Hi, Ben. You working on this James-Tyrell thing?"

"Yeah. I'd like to come around and talk, if you've got time."

I glanced at my watch. "I've got a class in five minutes, but my morning's free from ten o'clock on. How about coming by the office in about an hour?"

"I'll be there," he said, and we both hung up.

My class was only marginally successful, as the kids' minds and my own were more on our contemporary tragedy than on the devastating impact of the vigorous barbarian hordes on the declining Roman Empire in the West. I returned to my office wondering if we would not all have been better off if I had taken the suggestion of one of my pushier students and thrown the class open to a discussion of Marian James-Tyrell's demise.

I had just unlocked my office door when Ben rounded the corner and came down the hall. I had known Ben Latta for a little more than a year, since he had enrolled in my Western Civilization course in the evening division. In his early thirties, he projected an air of healthy anonymity; there was nothing remarkable about his appearance, but you knew somehow that if you had to call on him to perform a vigorous task he'd be able to handle it.

"Come on in and have a seat," I said, removing a couple of books from the stuffed chair and placing them on a relatively level space on my cluttered desk.

"Thanks, John," he said. He settled into the chair with a grateful sigh. "I'm beat," he said, and he looked it.

The heat of the day was beginning to build, so I wrestled with the one window my office possessed. When it was up as far as it would go, I sat down at my desk and looked across at Ben. His eyes were closed, and his features were stamped with fatigue.

I hadn't known he was a cop in the beginning. For most of the semester he'd just been one of several older students in the class. His questions were perceptive and his grades were uniformly excellent, but I'd come to expect a higher level of performance from my adult students than I got from most of the time-serving, college-aged kids, so there was nothing particularly remarkable about him.

Then one day he showed up at my office and wanted to talk about a matter of business—police business. One of my former students, who had had to drop out of college to make a living, had applied for a job with the police department and had given me as a reference, and Ben wanted to ask me some questions about him. A few weeks later Ben stayed late after class to pursue a question about the superb horsemanship of the Mongol hordes, and we continued the discussion over a couple of beers at a tavern just off campus. By the end of the semester we had become friends, playing racquetball a couple of times a week and getting together every so often for a few beers.

As he sat there, sagging into the comfortable old chair, he looked as though he could use a beer or two just then. Or a couple of days' sleep.

"Did you get to bed last night?" I asked after a few moments.

"Not yet," he replied, opening his eyes with an obvious effort, "though that's where I'm headed after I talk to you."

"I'm not sure I can tell you anything you haven't already learned from other people," I said. "I've been to a few parties at their house, but we're not close friends. Harrison is on one of the faculty committees that I serve on, but we don't talk much. Marian and I found ourselves on opposite sides in faculty meetings from time to time, and we've exchanged hostile comments, though nothing serious."

"Yeah," he said. "Everyone I've talked to this morning has claimed not to know much about the Jameses, or the James-Tyrells, or whatever the hell they were known as collectively. Let's just see if you can't add a bit to my meager collection of facts."

"Okay, Sherlock. Have at it."

2

When Ben left my office an hour later, he looked even worse than he had when he came in. And I couldn't see that he had gained anything from his efforts. I had told him everything I could remember about Marian and Harrison, then he had asked me several questions about Katherine Roeder.

"Katie?" I said with surprise when he first mentioned her name. "Why, Katie is everybody's sweetheart."

Ben pretended to misunderstand. "She's a bit old for you, isn't she?"

I ignored that and asked, "What do you want to know about her? She's somewhere in her fifties, I'd guess. She's a widow with two grown sons, and since the boys have been gone from home she's poured herself heart and soul into the college. She's been a member of the English department since God knows when."

I thought I could see what Ben was interested in, but I decided to let him come right out and ask me, which he did without any further sparring.

"What about bad feelings between her and Dr. James-Tyrell?"

"You're referring to the chairmanship thing?" I said in a

questioning tone, but Ben just sat there waiting for an answer. After a moment, I spoke.

"Well, you've got to understand about Katie. When her husband, Ted, died of cancer a dozen or so years back, she transferred all the love she had felt for him to the two other pillars of her life—her sons and Brookleigh College. And when the boys finished school and moved away, the college received all the attention that she had until then bestowed on her children. Even before this Katie had been a highly regarded faculty member, but once the boys were gone the college became the prime focus of her life. She is an outstanding teacher in the conventional mold, and until Marian joined the faculty it was assumed by everyone, including Katie herself, that she would succeed to the department chair when old Professor Burke finally retired."

I was sure that I wasn't telling Ben anything he hadn't heard before, but he didn't stop me so I just continued.

"And then Marian came along. You know how some people take an instant dislike to each other for no apparent reason whatever?"

Ben nodded.

"Well, it was like that with Katie and Marian. There was bad chemistry between them from the first day they met. Marian's dominant, assertive personality clashed with Katie's gentle and relaxed but no less effective way of doing things. In fact, Marian seemed to be about the only person or thing on earth capable of ruffling Katie's feathers.

"When Burke announced his intention to retire, Katie received a powerful shock when she learned that the chairmanship was not to become hers automatically as she had assumed. Rather, the administration announced that it would consider applications from within the department and at the same time would advertise the position nationally. Within a couple of weeks the school was deluged with letters of application from all over the United States and several foreign countries as well."

"Why all the interest?" Ben asked. "I know that Brookleigh is a pleasant school, but it's small and not very prestigious and, from grumbling remarks I've heard you make, I take it that the pay is not remarkable. So why should there have been so many applications?"

"Hell, Ben, college teaching positions in English, as well as

14

history and the other liberal arts, have been extremely scarce since the beginning of the seventies, and there are a great many holders of Ph.D.s outside of academia who stubbornly cling to the dream of teaching. They work at various jobs to keep body and soul together—driving cabs, pumping gas, clerking in grocery stores, and the like—but their main occupation in life is sending résumés to every college which might conceivably have an opening in their fields. The slightest hint brings them out in hordes, and they are joined by their more fortunate colleagues who already have teaching positions but want to move on to better schools."

Ben had some difficulty accepting the fact that there were vast numbers of highly educated individuals at large whose training was going to waste, and as I supplied him with statistics I thought about how close I had come to being one of them.

I had been very lucky. The history field was at least as hard-hit as English, and as I was putting the finishing touches on my dissertation I began to think that I might have been better off if I had chosen to become a janitor instead of a historian. As the job market got tighter, colleges became increasingly selective in filling openings. Not only were they able to hold out for degrees from the best universities, but they could virtually dictate the curriculum they expected from applicants and still have a large number to pick from. In the 1950s and early sixties, one could find a job at a decent university with only a master's and no experience whatever. Nowadays, even the worst colleges generally considered only those candidates with doctorates in hand, some teaching experience, published work, and several areas of competence.

It had been my good fortune that Brookleigh College had needed someone with precisely my qualifications at precisely the time that I entered the job market. My degree was from an excellent school, my grades were good, and—more important than I liked to think—the professor who directed my doctoral dissertation was a former classmate of the head of Brookleigh's history department. I got the job, probably as much on the strength of the Old Boy Network as on my own merits, and I had been there ever since. Despite my good fortune, or perhaps because of it, I sympathized deeply with those on the outside trying desperately to get in. Like the hundreds who applied for the English department opening.

After a few questions regarding the plight of the lumpen professoriate, Ben realized that it was a dead end and returned to the matter at hand.

"Get on with your story," he said tiredly.

"Sure. After spending several days trying to bring some order to the chaotic and ever-growing pile of applications, the dean decided to simplify his task by naming a new chairman from the existing staff and turning over to that lucky soul the onerous task of filling the vacancy thus created. Though several other members of the department had formally asked to be considered for the chairmanship, Katie and Marian were the only serious contenders. Katie had established her competence by more than twenty years of exemplary teaching and service on countless committees, and compared to her Marian was a virtual tyro. But Marian's brilliance was recognized even by those who disliked her personally, and, as far as professional qualifications were concerned, the contest between them ended in a dead heat."

"So how was it decided to give the job to Dr. James-Tyrell?" Ben asked.

"In the end," I replied, "what settled the matter was the administration's drive for a New Image—which appears in all intercampus communications with capitalized initial letters. Katie Roeder, with her middle-aged spread, graying hair, and fusty old suits, didn't have it; Marian James-Tyrell did."

"So Dr. James-Tyrell got the job that Dr. Roeder thought should have been hers. How did Dr. Roeder take it?"

"How do you think she took it?" I asked. "She took it very hard, and there were some sharp exchanges between the two women during faculty meetings for the next semester or so. After that, they adopted positions of cool, studied politeness toward each other, and I am unaware of any later overt clashes between them. All I can tell you for sure, Ben, is that Katie definitely had no love for her department chairman."

"Would you say that she hated her?"

I thought for a moment. "If by hate you mean intense dislike, then I suppose it is possible that Katie hated her. Probable, even. But I don't for a moment believe that she hated Marian enough to kill her, if that's what you're getting at. Besides, this happened years ago. If she were going to kill Marian she would have done it then, while the wound was fresh."

"Unless," Ben said, "she decided to divert suspicion from

herself by waiting until things cooled down and people began to discount the hard feelings between the two women—just as you are doing now."

"I'm not discounting them," I protested. "I'm saying they never were strong enough to produce a murder. Besides, Ben, you really don't believe that people are cold-blooded enough to wait for years to take revenge just to make it appear that they have no motive."

He looked at me sadly and said, "You'd probably be surprised what people are cold-blooded enough to do."

He thumbed through his notebook for a moment, then he looked up at me and asked, "What do you know about Kenneth Phillips?"

"Kenneth Phillips?" I asked, surprised. But Ben just stared at me, waiting for my answer.

"Just that he's an English major in his senior year at the college. You know him, Ben. He's that tall, good-looking kid who sits at the front of the room near the door in my British history survey class." Ben was taking that class as well. He nodded slightly and waited for me to continue.

"Well, I've had him in several other courses, and he's a pretty good student, despite his reluctance to take an active part in classroom discussions. Beyond that, I know nothing about him at all."

Ben looked back at his notebook again, and I took advantage of the pause to ask a question of my own. "Why all the questions about Dr. Roeder and Kenneth Phillips? Rumor has it that your people practically caught Harrison redhanded."

"Rumors," he snorted. "I'm just checking all the bases, trying to be thorough." He started to put his notebook away.

I leaned forward and put my elbows on the desk. "Listen, Ben," I said. "I know you're bushed, but can you just give me some idea of what happened? I've heard fourteen different versions, and each one has sounded more implausible than the one before."

He wanted to go home, I knew. If I had said to forget it, to go and get some rest, he would gladly have done so. He gave me a moment, hoping that my better nature would come to his rescue. When it didn't, he dropped back into the chair with a sigh that was almost a groan and said, "Goddamn it, John, this is police business." There was no heat in it, though, so I just waited.

"All right," he said at last. "What do you want to know?"

"Whatever you can tell me," I replied, trying hard to contain my surprise that he had given in to my request.

"Well," he began, "at 12:03 this morning Harrison James telephoned the station and reported that he had just found his wife dead. She had been murdered in her bed, he said, and her killer had made his escape through a bedroom window as James was coming upstairs after arriving home late from a rehearsal. A car was dispatched immediately and arrived at the Tyrell mansion within two minutes of the call. When Dr. James answered the front door he was obviously upset. In fact, the officers reported later that he was sobbing when they first saw him and that he had trouble speaking. He took them upstairs to his wife's bedroom, but he waited in the hall when they went in."

Ben rested his head on the back of the chair and half closed his eyes as he spoke. I suspected that he was going over these things as much to arrange them in his mind as to enlighten me, and I resolved to remain as still as possible so as not to break the spell.

"They found Dr. James-Tyrell lying on her back in her bed. The bed clothing was all twisted and disturbed, as though she had thrashed about a lot before dying. One pillow was in its normal position beneath her head; the other was lying on the floor near the foot of the bed. Her body was still warm, but she was obviously dead. She had no pulse and was not breathing, and her eyes were wide open, staring at the ceiling. The police dispatcher had called for an ambulance immediately after sending the patrol car, and it arrived a few minutes after my men got there. One of them went downstairs to let the EMTs in, and they confirmed that she was dead.

"I got there a few minutes later. Cox let me in, looking as though he was about to lose his supper—he's a new man, and this is his first homicide. I went directly upstairs, passed James, who was sitting on a chair in the hall looking stunned, and went into the bedroom. Except for the body, there were only two things of interest about the room. A nightstand which ordinarily stood at the head of the bed beneath the window had been overturned and apparently kicked out of the way—a lamp and several other items were fanned out on the floor in front of the window. And then the window itself—it was wide open, and the screen had been forced out of its frame and lay on the roof outside.

"After taking all this in, I went back into the hall and asked James if there was somewhere we could talk. He seemed a bit dazed, but he took me downstairs to a room filled with books and playbills and posters and such. We sat down and I asked him to tell me what had happened.

"He seemed to be holding himself together only with great effort, but he managed to give me a fairly coherent story. According to him, he had left a play rehearsal at the college at a few minutes before midnight and had driven straight home. After parking his car in the garage, he let himself in through the kitchen door with his key and was going up the stairs when he heard a crash in his wife's bedroom. He said that he was surprised at the sound but not unduly alarmed, since he assumed that his wife had merely overturned something by accident. Nevertheless, he called out her name and asked if she was all right. There was no answer, and another sound—apparently that of the screen being forced out—made him immediately anxious. He ran the rest of the way up the stairs and down the hall to his wife's room.

"The room was dark when he entered, but there was enough light coming through the open window for him to distinguish his wife's form on the bed with a pillow across her face. He rushed across and threw the pillow aside, only to see his wife's open, startled eyes, staring sightlessly at the ceiling. James said that he stood there for a few moments, looking down at his wife's dead face—he said that he knew instantly that she was dead—and then a noise from outside the window, like a heavy weight being dropped from a height, caused him to look out. A moment later he caught a glimpse of a dark figure running across the back lawn, away from the house. James said he couldn't tell whether it was a man or a woman, though he had a vague idea that it was a man. He then picked the phone up off the floor, called the report in to the station, and went downstairs to wait for the officers to arrive."

Ben seemed to have come to the end of his story, so I asked, "Do you believe him?"

"Well, no," he said, hesitantly. "That is, he gives every indication of being a bereaved husband, and there is other evidence which could support the idea of an intruder, but my feeling is that he makes a damned sight more likely murderer than some alleged mysterious stranger. At the moment, I'd have to say that things look pretty bad for Dr. James."

"What's this other evidence you mentioned?" I asked, hoping that he wouldn't clam up on me after going this far.

He gave me a long look, then with a faint smile and an almost imperceptible shake of the head he continued. "James's story suggests that someone broke into the house and surprised Dr. James-Tyrell in her bed, suffocating her with a pillow before she could raise an alarm. If that's what happened, it's unlikely that the intruder just walked in or had a key. If there was an intruder, he probably would have had to break in, and that should have left some evidence."

"I take it that you found such evidence?"

"Well, we found what *could* be evidence. On the other hand, it might mean nothing at all."

"What was it?" I asked.

"At the back of the Tyrell mansion is a small outside door at the bottom of a steep flight of steps which leads to the basement. The door itself is below ground level. We found that one of the glass panes in the door had been broken out—or, rather, broken in, since the glass shards lay inside the basement—and the door was unlocked. It rained heavily yesterday morning, you remember, but the scrap of carpet that lay just inside the door—where it should have been soaked by the rain—was completely dry, so it appears that the window could not have been broken before then. If there was an intruder, he could have gotten into the house that way. The door is far enough away from Dr. James-Tyrell's bedroom that she might not have heard the sound of the glass breaking."

I thought for a moment, then I asked, "What about the supposed intruder's departure? Is there any evidence to support James's story that the killer left through the second-floor window?"

"Aside from the window being open and the screen off when the officers arrived—which James could have done himself— there isn't any. There were no useable finger prints on the window itself or, for that matter, on the basement door. If there was an intruder, he must have used gloves."

"How about outside the window?"

"There's a short stretch of roof and then the stone patio below. If someone had dropped from the roof, he would not necessarily have left marks on the stone. At any rate, we didn't find any."

"How about on the lawn itself?"

"When I got there the patrolmen had not gone outside the house. I kept them inside until I finished questioning James, then I took a look outside. There were some switches inside the back door, and I played around with them until I found which ones controlled the outside lights. There were enough lights to illuminate the entire patio area and about fifty feet of lawn beyond it. Farther out, it was all black. I sent the men out with flashlights to see if they could find any sign of an intruder, cautioning them to watch where they were stepping so as not to destroy any evidence that might be there. Maybe I should have kept them on the patio until daylight, to be sure that they didn't mess up anything, but we couldn't just sit there and assume that the intruder, if there was one, had gotten clean away. Hell, he might have been sitting out there in the dark, watching us. The men checked all around the back, in the carriage house and in the gazebo, but in the dark they couldn't find anything. After it got light this morning I went out and looked again, and I did find one place where the hedges were fairly thin which looked like someone might have pushed his way through fairly recently, but there is no way of telling just when in the past couple of days it happened."

"Were there no tracks on the patio or in the house? From dew on the intruder's feet, I mean?"

"No. According to the meteorology department here at the college, dew didn't fall until after four this morning. And, of course, it's been so dry here lately that the ground had soaked up every bit of yesterday morning's rainfall in just a couple of hours."

I shook my head. I still couldn't accept the idea that Harrison was a murderer.

"Are you going to keep Harrison locked up?" I asked.

"That's up to the prosecuting attorney. He and James's lawyer were in conference the last I heard." Ben pushed himself wearily to his feet and said, sarcastically, "If there's nothing else you need to know, I think I'll go try to get a few hours' sleep."

I grinned my thanks. He stopped short in the doorway and said, "I'll have to miss class tonight, teacher. I'm going to be busy." Then he stumbled out the door.

3

The phone was ringing when I got back to the office after my two-o'clock class. I unlocked the door hurriedly, dumped my books and notes into the chair, and leaned across the desk to answer it.

"Forest," I said.

"John, this is Corinne." Her voice was cool, which was no more than I would have expected. In fact, I was surprised that she was calling at all, since the last time we'd been together she had breathed new life into the old if-I-never-see-you-again-it-will-be-too-soon cliché.

"Yes?" I replied, matching her coolness.

"This isn't a personal call, John, it's business. I'm assigned to the James-Tyrell murder, and, bastard though you are, you are my only contact there on campus."

So it wasn't a coolness contest she was after. Beneath the thorns I detected an olive branch of sorts, because I knew—and Corinne knew that I knew—that a number of other people on campus would quite willingly have given her all the information she wanted. If I were so tactless as to point this out, however, Corinne would hang up and call one of them, and it really would be never before she spoke to me again. This was her way of reopening communications without having to take responsibility for doing so. It was up to me whether we took it any further. Crafty woman, that Corinne. Which was one of the things that attracted me to her. Hers was not the vixenish craftiness which many women coyly employ, but good old down-to-earth, hard-ball craftiness, of the kind you find in labor negotiators, con men, and politicians. And, for that matter, good journalists.

Though she was the one who had walked out on me, at that time I hadn't had the slightest desire to try to stop her. We were both pretty well fed up with each other. Since then I had cooled down considerably, but—despite the odd little twinge I felt inside on hearing her voice again—I wasn't certain whether I wanted to grasp the olive branch she was tentatively offering. So I moderated my coolness only slightly and answered her questions as formally as I would those of a stranger.

As I filled her in on the background, my mind flipped idly through the pages of my memory. Corinne Blakely worked as a general-assignment reporter for the Brookleigh *Ledger*, our afternoon daily. We had met several years before, when she was doing a piece on strained relations between the faculty and the administration at Brookleigh College. The president of the school, ably assisted by his dean, had launched a campaign to relieve the faculty of the tiresome responsibility of having any say whatever in the school's operations outside of the classroom—by such unsubtle means as establishing the agenda for and presiding over faculty meetings, for example—and I had become spokesman for the faculty position more or less by default.

That is, I was the only one willing to be identified as being steadfastly opposed to the inroads the administration was making into faculty rights. The other members of the faculty generally supported my position, but none wanted to be on the front lines, so I found myself out there alone, with my colleagues providing what support they could from a comfortably anonymous distance. The conflict grew acrimonious, and for a time it was touch and go whether I would keep my job, but at length a compromise of sorts was reached. It was not wholly satisfactory to either side, but it was something both could accept without excessive loss of face or sacrifice of principle. I kept my job, and in fact the president and I got along much better after it was all over than we had before it began. I still thought he was a reactionary tyrant, and he still regarded me as a dangerous would-be usurper of his rightful powers, but we both came out of our battles with respect for each other's abilities.

Corinne came on the scene as the conflict was winding down, and I wasn't at all eager to start it up again by making inflamatory remarks to a member of the press. As a result, our first meeting ended on a fairly sour note; she wanted information for her story, but I wouldn't play ball. Even so, I was impressed with the attractiveness of her appearance and her personality. I was still faithfully, if not happily, married at the time, but that didn't keep me from noticing.

Partly as a result of my involvement in the faculty-administration struggle, my wife, Shirley, decided to bail out of our marriage. It had been pretty rocky from the start, and when Shirley realized just how little history professors make, and how little job security junior faculty members have, she decided she didn't love me after all. She forced a division of property which made me sell the house and the car, then she took the money and ran. Within six months she had married a rising young insurance salesman in another town and had found true love in a mock-Tudor quasi-mansion with stable space for a Mercedes stallion and a Cadillac mare.

The breakup of the marriage had hurt me a lot less than I would have expected, so perhaps I hadn't loved her very much either. After the dust settled, all I felt toward her was massive indifference, tinged with a bit of resentment that she had dealt my financial well-being a rather heavy blow. Living solely on my salary and paying her alimony had forced me to take Draconian measures of frugality. I had to learn to do without a car and took up residence in a third-floor apartment above a funeral establishment. When Shirley's remarriage—for which I was profoundly thankful—freed me from the alimony albatross, I discovered that I had come to like not having to worry about rising gasoline prices, automobile insurance rates, and thugs who get their jollies out of slashing tires and breaking out car windows. The apartment was within easy walking distance of the campus, even on the coldest winter days, and I found a grocer who would deliver my weekly order of food with a smile, believe it or not.

So I settled into a comfortable bachelorhood. Then, a couple of months before Marian James-Tyrell's death, I had run into Corinne again at one of those tedious cocktail parties the college president's wife liked to spring on faculty and staff several times a year. Ordinarily, I avoided those gatherings religiously, but Mrs. Wilkerson's telephoned invitation had caught me with my excuses down and I had had no choice, short of brutal honesty, but to accept. I went fully prepared to be miserable, and of course I was, until Mrs. Wilkerson introduced me to an attractive brunette, saying, "Here, Corinne. Dr. Forest is by himself. Why don't you have him get you a drink?" before bustling off again.

There was something familiar about her, but I didn't place her until she said, "What are you doing here? Spying out the enemy camp?"

I laughed, remembering then, and asked if she had been promoted to society editor.

"That's not funny," she said with mock sternness. "And it certainly wouldn't be a promotion. I came because your illustrious leader has been named to one of the Governor's task forces on higher education and this was the only time he could see me for an interview before leaving for a week at the state capital. And now," she added ruefully, "his wife tells me he had to leave sooner than expected to attend a private meeting with the Governor."

"Well," I said, "at least you'll get a few free drinks out of it."

She snorted. "What I'd like to have is a nice, cold beer, but that humble drink would clearly be uncomfortable in this company." She cast an amused glance at the still-full glass of sherry I had been pretending to sip at ever since my arrival. I detest sherry, but Mrs. Wilkerson seemed to think it was the drink of choice among academic types and had neglected to provide any alternative.

"If it's beer you want," I said, thankfully placing my untasted glass on a marble mantlepiece, "Hobie's Tavern is just a couple of blocks from here, and I'll be happy to show my appreciation for the efforts of you hard-working defenders of the public's right to know by springing for a pint or two."

She eyed me speculatively. Hobie's was a respectable establishment with a bar at one end and a restaurant at the other. I had named it in hopes that the nature of the establishment would allay any suspicions that the abruptness of my approach might have produced. I am hopelessly old-fashioned in some ways.

She said, after only a moment's hesitation, "You're on. I've got my own car. Shall I meet you there?"

"Actually," I said with a grin, "you might consider giving me a lift. Among the many faults which stand in the way of my ever being named All-American Boy of the Year is the fact that I don't own an automobile."

She raised one eyebrow, which I'd never seen a woman do before, and said, "How quaint. Do you also manage without a television?"

"No," I confessed, "I've got a TV, though I don't watch it much except for news programs and PBS."

"Well, that's something, anyway."

She looked around the room, spotted our hostess, and said to me, "Shall we go?"

We made our excuses—Corinne told Mrs. Wilkerson that, since her husband had had to leave, I had offered to fill her in on the president's background—and went out to her car, which was parked at the curb. As we walked along the sidewalk, I said, "You shouldn't have said that to Mrs. Wilkerson. Now she won't be able to enjoy the rest of her party for worrying about what horrible distortions I may be feeding you about her husband."

"Don't worry about Mrs. Wilkerson," Corinne replied. "She's not as scatter-brained as she looks."

We had several beers, sitting at a table in one of Hobie's dimly lit corners, and talked for a while about the inconsequentialities men and women talk about when they begin to realize that their interest in each other might possibly develop beyond the level of mere acquaintanceship.

After an hour that seemed much shorter, Corinne glanced at her watch and said, "I've got to be going. I'm covering a trial in the morning, so I won't be able to spend much time in the office, and I've got to knock out a piece on Wilkerson's appointment before I go home tonight. It shouldn't take long, since I don't know much more than what's in the press release, but if I don't write it tonight it won't get in tomorrow's paper. Can I give you a lift home?"

Ordinarily I would have said no. I had rediscovered the pleasures of walking and had begun to regard short trips in automobiles as needless indulgences. It was only eight blocks to my apartment, and the evening had been pleasant when we entered the tavern. I was, therefore, surprised to hear my voice saying, "Sure. I'd appreciate it."

I left some bills on the table, and we went out to her car. I gave her the address and we drove there in a comfortable silence. When we pulled up in front of the funeral home she raised her eyebrow at me again.

I laughed and said, "At least I don't have to worry about disturbing the downstairs neighbors."

She gave me a smile that was more than my feeble joke deserved and said, "Thanks for the beer. The working press appreciates it."

As I opened the door and slid out I said, "Always happy to help out the guardians of public liberty. I might even do it again sometime."

Her response was less concrete than I would have liked.

"You might," she said lightly, then she sped away down the street.

That had been the start.

Corinne's voice brought me back to the present. "Can't you hear me, John? Do we have a bad connection?"

"No, Corinne. I'm sorry. I was thinking about something else. What were you saying?"

She asked a few more questions before she rang off. Then I sat there for a time, considering whether I wanted to take advantage of this feeble beginning to try to rebuild our relationship.

4

As do most things in life, teaching in the evening has both good and bad aspects. On the good side, by scheduling one of my courses at night and concentrating the others on Mondays, Wednesdays, and Fridays, I was able to have Tuesdays and Thursdays all to myself. This was useful, since I had discovered back in graduate school that I did my best research and writing when I wasn't worrying about appointments or classes. I could get more work done in one uninterrupted day than I could in a week of half days.

On the bad side, my Wednesday workday didn't end until about nine-thirty in the evening, and a three-hour class can be tough to take after a full day of work. That was, of course, as true for my students as it was for me, so I tried doubly hard to make the time pass as pleasantly as possible for all parties.

Those students, by the way, were another plus for teaching at night. Since evening courses at Brookleigh College were an integral part of the college's offerings and not, as at some schools, a separate curriculum offered principally for evening and adult students, night classes had a large percentage of regular students. But added to the regular complement were people from the community at large—people who were store clerks, bank tellers, nurses, and the like during the day, but who became students when night fell. Some of them were working toward degrees, either for advancement at their present jobs or as a means of gaining entrée to other professions. Others were there simply because they wanted to learn, and that motivation is so rare today that it should be cherished by any teacher lucky enough to encounter it. With most kids regarding time spent in college much like prison time—to be put in until their four-year sentences are up—a teacher quickly learns to value the student who is happy to be there.

That semester my evening class was a survey of British history, one of those courses in which a couple of thousand years of history are covered in about fifty classroom hours, and the discussion of the Hundred Years' War and the Wars of the Roses had taken up most of that Wednesday evening's class time.

With a few good students interested enough to do the reading and develop opinions of their own, a class sometimes can almost teach itself. That's the way it had been that evening, and I hated to cut it off. But my voice was getting weak, and I could see that the long day was beginning to tell on some of the students as well. I sought to wrap things up.

"Edward IV's unexpected death at the age of forty-two," I began in my best don't-despair-the-end-is-near voice, "set the stage for one of the most dramatic and mysterious events in the history of England: the accession to the throne of Richard III and the subsequent disappearance of the two princes in the Tower, and we'll go into that next week. Richard, as we discussed earlier, had been his brother's most faithful servant throughout Edward's reign, but with Edward dead Richard revealed a side of his nature which had not until then manifested itself. It is possible, indeed, that Richard had never aspired to be king, but when circumstances presented him with the opportunity to seize the throne he apparently found himself unable to resist. Just how it all came about we'll get into at our meeting next week. In the meantime—"

"Dr. Forest?"

It was John DeLancy Warren, as he insisted on signing his papers, one of the brightest students I'd had in years. Unfortunately, he was also one of the most arrogant and obnoxious. He was wearing what I had come to think of as his uniform: badly scuffed shoes, suit trousers, and a long-sleeved white shirt with the cuffs loosely rolled up to just below his elbows. He was not afraid of hard work, and that, coupled with his considerable intelligence, put him well ahead of most of his classmates— and, as he sometimes gave evidence of thinking, ahead of his teachers as well. If he learned to keep his arrogance in check, and if someone didn't punch him out while he was learning, he might develop into a fine scholar.

"Yes, Warren? What is it?"

"You seem to be suggesting, Dr. Forest, that there was something unlawful or underhanded about Richard's becoming king. Isn't it a fact, however, that Richard was the rightful heir to the throne, since the sons of his brother Edward were bastards? And isn't it a further fact that the negative image of Richard that has been passed down from generation to generation is the result of a deliberate conspiracy on the part of professional historians from the time of the Tudors down to the present?"

"Are those facts, Mr. Warren?"

"I think they are, sir."

"And what, exactly, is your source for those facts?"

Warren hesitated slightly, but his voice when he spoke had lost none of its confidence. "Certainly not a history book, Dr. Forest, since the profession appears to have joined ranks pretty solidly behind the Richard-as-monster thesis."

There were noises from the other students in the class, some sharply drawn breaths and some snickers, and Warren looked pleased with the response.

"What, then, Mr. Warren?" I asked.

"Well, sir, for one thing there is Josephine Tey's novel, *The Daughter of Time*, in which she quite effectively destroys the edifice that the noble practitioners of your profession have erected down through the years."

I glanced at my watch. "It's almost nine-thirty, and we don't have time tonight even to begin to give the Richard III question the attention it deserves, but perhaps, since he seems to be primed to the gills with pro-Richard propaganda, Mr. Warren will whet our appetites for what is to come by giving us a quick rundown of the Richardist position. How about it, Mr. Warren?"

Warren tried without complete success to look surprised, but he had clearly been angling for a chance to show his stuff and his pleasure showed through plainly. "Why, yes, Dr. Forest. I'll be happy to give it a try."

"Good," I said. "Come on up to the desk."

As he gathered up some notes, I said to the class, "The foremost modern proponent of the Richardist school was the British mystery novelist Josephine Tey, who embodied most of the pro-Richardist arguments in the novel to which Mr. Warren has made reference and which, presumably, he will be enlightening us on momentarily."

I went over to an empty chair, and Warren took my place behind the lectern. Spreading his notes before him, he cleared his throat and began.

"First—for those who may be completely unfamiliar with the history of Richard and the princes—a few comments on the nature of the traditional case against Richard III. The official party line, so to speak, is that Richard was a monster, deformed in body and in mind, who deliberately and heartlessly murdered his two young nephews in order to seize the throne of England for himself. This version is based on three sources, none of them contemporary with the events they purport to describe. One is an account written by Polydore Virgil, a historian in the pay of Henry Tudor, who seized the throne of England after Richard's defeat and death at the Battle of Bosworth Field in the summer of 1485. Another is an account which historians have for centuries attributed to Sir Thomas More but which, as Josephine Tey points out, was actually written by Richard's most bitter enemy, John Morton, bishop of Ely. And the last is Shakespeare's play, *The Tragedy of King Richard the Third*, written a century after Richard's death—during the reign of Henry VII's granddaughter Elizabeth I—and itself based on the first two sources.

"Written, as they were, under the Tudors, whose very presence on the throne was made possible only by the overthrow of Richard, these accounts naturally seek to portray Richard in the worst possible light. That, plus the fact that none of them are contemporary or eyewitness accounts, should make them suspect in anyone's eyes. For some reason, however, professional historians have accepted this tainted version from the beginning and have with rare unanimity held on to it doggedly ever since, suppressing or distorting every bit of evidence which does not support their case. Maybe their persistence in adhering to this false version arises from a human, though unprofessional, reluctance to admit that they have made an error, but whatever their reason, historians have conspired down through the centuries to present a false picture of Richard III and the events with which his name has been unalterably linked. The truth, as Josephine Tey makes amply clear, is really quite simple and straightforward, and when one looks at the evidence it is clear that the traditional version just does not stand up to objective examination. The facts are simply stated."

Warren was enjoying himself. I was impressed by the amount of care he had obviously put into preparing his case, especially since he'd had no way of knowing that he would have an opportunity to make a formal presentation to the class. I had expected him to baldly state the principal Richardist positions and then sit down, but he was clearly prepared for a detailed presentation. He had the attention of the class, and he was doing a good job of keeping it. I reflected again that he had the potential of developing into an excellent teacher—if he didn't annoy someone into killing him in the meantime. I listened as he continued.

"Throughout the reign of his brother Edward IV, Richard, duke of Gloucester, had served the king faithfully and well, and when Edward died on April 9, 1483, his will named Richard as protector of the king's twelve-year-old son and successor, Edward V. Edward IV's queen, Elizabeth, was a member of the parvenu Woodville family, whose members had capitalized greatly on their royal connections while Edward was alive and planned to do so even more now that he was dead by gaining control of the young and impressionable Edward V and manipulating him for their own benefit. To do this, they attempted to subvert the terms of Edward IV's will by seizing control of the government and preventing Richard from performing his duties as lord protector. But Richard moved faster and arrested a good many of the Woodville faction who were plotting against him. Some of the faction managed to escape abroad, and Edward's widow obtained sanctuary at Westminster for herself and her younger son, Richard, duke of York, who was only nine years old.

"With his enemies out of the way for the time being, Richard, who had taken custody of young Edward V on April 30, faithfully carried out his duties as lord protector and proceeded with preparations for the coronation of the young king. On the sixteenth of June he secured the release of Richard of York from his mother's custody so that he could play his part in the upcoming coronation and so that the brothers could have the pleasure of each other's company."

Warren paused, apparently for effect, before continuing in a more intense voice.

"Meanwhile, Richard's enemies had continued to plot against him. Fortunately, a secret meeting of this cabal was discovered, and Richard had the plotters—Lords Stanley and Hastings and the bishop of Ely, John Morton—arrested. Generous and forgiving man that he was, Richard allowed Morton and Stanley to go free, but Hastings, the ringleader, was tried and found guilty of treason, and he was executed a week after his arrest.

"Up to this point, all of Richard's actions had been motivated solely by a desire to promote and protect the interests of his nephew Edward, whom he regarded as the rightful king of England. But sometime in June, Robert Stillington, bishop of Bath and Wells, revealed to Parliament that at the time of Edward's marriage to Elizabeth Woodville he was already married to Lady Eleanor Butler. This made Edward's children by Elizabeth Woodville bastards and thus ineligible for succession to the throne. Parliament accepted Stillington's evidence and incorporated it into an act called Titulus Regius, which also named Richard the legitimate successor to Edward IV. Parliament then petitioned Richard to accept the crown, which he reluctantly did on June 26. Afterwards, Richard had the two princes confined to the Tower for their own protection and to keep them from being used against him by his enemies, and there they remained, alive and well, throughout Richard's reign."

As Warren paused again to shuffle through his notes, I glanced around the room. Despite the lateness of the hour, he was holding his audience well. I looked back at him as he continued.

"When, on August 22, 1485, Richard was killed at Bosworth Field in the battle between his Yorkist forces and the Lancastrian forces of Henry Tudor, control of the princes passed into the hands of Henry, who began to rule as Henry VII. Henry quickly consolidated his control over England by marrying Elizabeth, the eldest daughter of Edward IV, by locking up Elizabeth Woodville in a convent, by having the Titulus Regius repealed and all copies of it destroyed, and by murdering off all the Yorkist claimants to the throne, beginning with the two princes in the Tower, whom he caused to be murdered between June 16 and July 16, 1486. We can be fairly certain of these dates, because the man to whom Henry entrusted the deed received a general pardon on the sixteenth of June, 1486, and then received another general pardon exactly one month later. There can have been no reason for the issuance of a second general pardon, unless he had in the intervening month committed some serious crime for which Henry was instantly pardoning him. Clearly, that crime was the murder of the two princes.

"Naturally, Henry did not want the people to know that he had had the princes killed, so, to account for their absence, he promoted the story that they had been murdered by their uncle, Richard III. Conveniently for Henry, Richard was not there to defend himself, and the Tudor version of the story of Richard III and the princes in the Tower was accepted and promoted by historians from that day until this. In fact, until Josephine Tey's *Daughter of Time* was published in 1951, only three vindications of Richard III had ever been written—by men named Buck, Walpole, and Markham in the seventeenth, eighteenth, and nineteenth centuries respectively. Aside from those isolated instances, the conspiracy against Richard has been remarkably successful for nearly five hundred years." Warren shot me a smirking glance with that, then returned his attention to the class.

"Those are the facts in the case. There are also some persuasive conclusions that can be drawn from them and from what we know of the people and the times. There is, for example, the matter of Richard's character. Throughout his brother's reign, Richard had been Edward's most faithful and loyal subject. It is completely out of keeping with what we know about Richard to think that he could have been a faithful brother with no desire to seize the throne up until Edward's death, and then could suddenly have come to desire the throne so much that he was willing to murder his own nephews in order to get it. Why, indeed, should he have usurped it at all? Under the terms of Edward's will, Richard was lord protector of England until young Edward was old enough to rule for himself. Richard was, in fact, already king in everything but name, and he was the kind of person who would have been quite happy continuing to serve his brother, through his son, for as long as his services were needed.

"It was not until he learned from the evidence presented to Parliament by Bishop Stillington that the young princes were illegitimate and thus debarred from sitting on the throne that he had any thought whatever of taking the throne for himself. And even then he did not do so until it was actually offered to him by an act of Parliament.

"Once on the throne, he served as one of England's most just and able kings. He kept the princes safe and secure in the Tower, where they could not be manipulated against him, and he ruled the country capably until his life and throne were taken from him at Bosworth Field.

"The traditional version, promoted by professional historians, paints Richard in the blackest of hues, but it does so without the slightest shred of evidence. Virtually the whole of the traditional case rests upon *The History of King Richard the Third*, which the historians claim was written by Sir Thomas More. Even if that claim were true—which it isn't—the book would be suspect, since More was only a small child at the time these events took place and was not privy to them. In fact, however, the author of this scurrilous attack on Richard was none other than John Morton, bishop of Ely, who had plotted against Richard and finally fled into exile, to return only after Richard was dead. But writing this lying account was not the only thing that Morton did to besmirch Richard's name. Even before he fled from England he tried, unsuccessfully, to spread the rumor that Richard had murdered the princes. The rumor was recorded in a contemporary chronicle, but it obviously was not widespread, since Richard made no effort to squelch it. Morton also spread the rumor on the Continent, and it was mentioned by Chancellor Gaillaume de Rochefort in the French estates-general in January, 1484. There was, of course, no substance to the rumor—it was entirely the product of Morton's vengeful spitefulness.

"The fact of the matter is that there is no evidence whatever to support the accusations which historians have levelled against Richard for five centuries. His defamation was from the beginning a tissue of lies promoted by historians without the slightest foundation in fact, and it is high time that the story was set straight. Since professional historians won't do it, it is up to honest lay people like Josephine Tey to spread the truth."

With that, Warren gathered up his notes and returned to his seat.

Back at the lectern, I said, "Thank you, Mr. Warren, for that admirable presentation of the Richardist position. You've certainly given us all a lot to think about until we meet again next week.

Before then, however, perhaps some of you would like to look a bit further into some of the points Mr. Warren has raised. Are there others in the class who have been seduced by Miss Tey's little book?"

Several hands were raised. I made a number of assignments, first to those who had raised their hands, and then to other students who had shown an interest in the period. By the time I was through, a third of the class had specific assignments for the next week, and I suggested that the remaining students read what they could find on the subject and come to class prepared to thrash the question out.

"Perhaps," I said as the class prepared to go home for the night, "we'll be able to arrive at some sort of consensus on the 'facts' of this interesting case next week."

I followed the last of the students into the hallway, flipping out the lights in the classroom as I passed the switch. Outside the building, the night was fine and clear, and as I stood in the cool, quiet air I thought about all the mischief Josephine Tey had caused with her *Daughter of Time*.

People, as even the most casual observer cannot help but notice, are not just willing to be gulled—they are eager. They reject the rational and the concrete in favor of the fanciful and the fantastic. They view facts and scientific evidence with great disdain, if not outright disbelief, while they enthusiastically embrace the most outrageous inventions of charlatans and madmen. There are still some people who insist that the entire space program, from the landings on the moon and Mars to the fly-bys of the outer planets, has been a gigantic hoax, perpetrated on the nation and the world by the scientific community for some obscure reason of its own. Mountains of hard scientific evidence are as nothing to them. Yet there are people—there is considerable overlap here—who are willing to accept a few large-scale designs scratched out on a plain in South America as incontrovertible proof that the earth has been visited by extraterrestrial beings, or who see the very existence of the pyramids as adequate evidence of non-human involvement in mankind's early history.

Things which appeal to the popular imagination are immediately and fervently accepted on the basis of the most flimsy and even nonexistent evidence, while unpleasant or unromantic truths are required to meet the most rigorous scientific tests, and then are *still* rejected. A new wave of know-nothingism has arrived, and the so-called common wisdom has gained ascendancy. People believe in conspiracies behind virtually every assassination, even after exhaustive investigations fail to produce the slightest shred of proof; they believe in flying saucers, despite the total lack of physical evidence for them; and they believe, on the basis of nothing more than the disgruntled complaints of a few special-pleading amateurs, that the historical profession has conspired for half a millennium to hide the truth about the princes in the Tower.

I shook my head over the perversity of the human creature and then started to walk home. As I walked, I let my mind wander where it would, and, not surprisingly, I found myself thinking about Marian's death. It was still early and I had nothing else to do for the evening, so I decided to indulge my curiosity and stroll past her house.

5

The Tyrell mansion enjoyed pride of place in Brookleigh. Located in the best section of town, it was surrounded by other houses of the same sort, only less grand. There had been some commercial encroachment into the neighborhood, but it had been tastefully done. Only two short blocks from the Tyrell place a group of handsome homes had been converted into offices for doctors, lawyers, dentists, architects, and the like. The posh setting had been a real boon for the businesses, though the residents of the area had not been overjoyed at the development. For one thing, parking on the streets had become virtually impossible in the daytime because of the great influx of automobiles. But the professional invasion had been discreetly accomplished, and the only outward evidence that these were not residences were the ubiquitous plaques beside their front doors which listed the various offices housed within.

As I walked past I noticed that most had lights on in various rooms, probably left on to discourage break-ins; somehow I doubted that doctors, lawyers, dentists, and the like kept such late hours.

Cops do, however, and the sight of a phone booth in front of one of the grander commercialized mansions made me think about phoning Ben to ask if there had been any new developments in Marian's murder. I had called him often enough over the past year to set up racquetball games that I didn't need to look up the number, so I left the door of the booth open as I fished in my pocket for some change. A faint whizzing noise caught my attention just as I was dropping the coin into the slot, and I looked around to see what it was. Twenty feet away, in the bright light shed by a corner streetlamp, a refined-looking white toy poodle was relieving himself with great dignity on one of the legs of a square mail box. His task finished, he gave me an arch glance and then pranced off into the darkness with that arrogant, jaunty little trot on which poodles appear to hold a patent.

My delay in dialing a number appeared to upset the telephone, which began to make peculiar noises, so I hung up, retrieved my coin, and started over again from scratch. It was to no avail, however, for the night sergeant informed me that, while Ben was still on duty, he was out of the station, and the sergeant didn't know when he would be back or where he could be reached. I hung up and proceeded on to my destination.

The Tyrell estate occupied an entire block by itself. The main house was set forward and a little to the left of center as you faced it from the front. As I walked slowly along the sidewalk, I could see that the house was completely dark. A full moon provided a great deal of illumination, so I had little difficulty picking out details in the night. I was already generally familiar with the layout from having attended a few parties at the mansion, but somehow the fact that Marian had been murdered there made it seem subtly different.

To the right and a bit to the rear of the main house stood the carriage house in which Marian and Harrison had lived until her mother's death. Since then the building had been used as a guest house and, of course, for garaging cars underneath. A paved driveway essed its way through the trees to the carriage house, and I gave in to temptation and walked quietly up the drive, first ascertaining that there was no one in sight to observe my act of trespass.

The night was very quiet, its silence broken only by subdued animal and insect sounds and the occasional, distant noise of a large truck chugging down one of the major traffic arteries many blocks away. The neighborhood had virtually no nighttime traffic, except police patrol cars which glided respectfully and regularly through the wealthy streets, providing discreet protection for the fortunate citizens living there.

This thought made me mindful of the foolishness of my behavior. If I were caught on the grounds of the Tyrell estate in the dead of night I might have some difficulty persuading the authorities that my only reason for being there was curiosity. For a moment I considered leaving, but then I realized that I was just as likely to be observed leaving right away, before I had a look, as I would be if I left later after a quick turn around the estate. As I intended to stay on paved surfaces, I didn't think I would disturb any remaining evidence, and the fact that the estate was surrounded on three sides by a tall green wall of hedges meant that there was no danger of my being observed from the streets beyond.

An inlaid stone pathway connected the carriage house to the patio at the rear of the mansion. From the patio I looked out over the immense back yard. Toward the rear of the estate on the right sat a large gazebo, and in the corresponding position on the left was a tiny lake stocked with lily pads and goldfish. A decorative bridge spanned the lake's narrowest dimension. Connecting everything was a cobblestone path which meandered from the rear of the main house, around the gazebo, across to the lake, and then back to the house. Stately old trees, standing singly and in groups, combined with wide expanses of manicured lawns and strategically located flower beds to give it all a park-like air. With its convoluted twists and turns, the route described by the path could take as much as ten minutes to navigate at a leisurely pace.

Without consciously deciding to do so, I started down the path toward the gazebo. As I walked, I reflected that the cost of maintaining the place must be enormous. Just keeping the lawn mowed, the flower beds neat and orderly, the hedges trimmed, and the walkway clipped must have been enough to keep two gardeners employed full time from early spring to late fall. Add another man to handle repairs and maintenance on the house and outbuildings and a couple of maids inside, and the household payroll must have come to considerably more than Harrison and Marian together brought home from their teaching jobs. Apparently old man Tyrell had left quite a pile, because there was never any hint that the Jameses were strapped for funds.

Some of my associates with socialist inclinations grumbled a bit about the estate being wasteful, and perhaps they were right. Still, it seemed to me that it would be a shame not to keep up such a lovely, picture-book place. Had the Jameses been reclusive, had they hoarded that beauty all to themselves, I might have been less sympathetic, but in fact they made it available for guided tours at no charge, and Marian regularly hosted charitable fetes on the back lawn. All in all, I thought that Marian and Harrison had set a good example of being wealthy without being offensive about it. Too bad most rich people don't behave the same way.

Even if it was conspicuous consumption to spend fifty thousand or so a year on household help, the community benefited far more than if the Jameses had let the place go to seed and prudently put what they saved thereby into money-market instruments. Five local citizens made adequate if unspectacular livings keeping the place up; the community had a tourist attraction that drew people from the surrounding states; and the Jameses had an idyllic place in which to live. I couldn't see that anyone suffered by it.

As I passed an exotic-looking flowering bush that hugged the side of the pathway, a whiff of jasmine triggered a vivid memory of my last visit here a month or two before. Marian and Harrison frequently invited faculty members and their spouses or dates for dinner and drinks, either individually or in small groups, and once each year they held a large outdoor buffet for the entire faculty and staff of the college. I had taken Corinne to the most recent one, and the tantalizing smell evoked a powerful image of Marian as she had looked that afternoon, strolling along the pathway on President Wilkerson's arm. She was wearing a fluffy dress in lovely, soft colors, which floated about her body like a mist, and her black hair was done in a style which managed to look wind-blown and perfect at the same time. Altogether, she was as beautiful as I had ever seen her.

Come to think of it, Marian had seemed subtly different that afternoon and on those few occasions since that I had been around her. She had always been an attractive woman who was completely in command of her life and at ease with the world around her, but that afternoon she seemed younger and more girlish than the Marian I had known for years. She even giggled in response to a remark Wilkerson made to her as Corinne and I passed them on the pathway—something about "damned revolutionaries," if I heard him right. I was relieved to see that he accompanied the remark with a grin and a wink in my direction.

But she'll never laugh again, I thought with sadness as I stood there in the quiet night, breathing the scented, memory-laden air. To shake off the melancholia which was threatening to overcome me, I resumed my walk down the path.

I had just passed the gazebo and turned toward the lake when a flicker of light back at the main house caught my eye. I was not sure at first whether I had actually seen anything, but my uncertainty disappeared a moment later when another faint flash of light appeared in one of the second-floor windows. I wasn't familiar with the mansion's upstairs layout, but it seemed likely that the light had been in Marian's bedroom.

My first impulse was to call the police. I have never been able to understand those citizens of fact and fiction who rush headlong into the apprehension of evil-doers without establishing whether the cops can handle the problem. What I needed was a phone. The main house was obviously out—I wasn't about to go in there and phone for help while the prowler was standing just a few feet above my head. There was the public phone I had used a few minutes before, but in the darkness I couldn't see any way through the hedges, and even if I managed to find a way off the estate without alerting the prowler, the phone was still a block or two away, and whoever was in the house could get clean away in my absence. That left the carriage house. I figured there was a chance it had a working phone, or at least an extension, and I had just decided to try slipping inside quietly to make the call when a figure appeared at what I took to be Marian's window.

I was in a fix. I was standing out in the open on the pathway, halfway between two clumps of trees about a hundred feet apart. It seemed unlikely that the person in the window could see me at that distance, but if I moved at all he would certainly spot me.

I noticed some faint movement at the window, and then he was out on the roof, scrambling down toward the edge. In that moment I looked desperately around for some cover. The trees were too distant to be useful, but a flower bed stretched along the house side of the path a few feet away, so I dove down beside it, hoping that the man's preoccupation with getting off the roof would keep him from noticing my movement, and also hoping that, once he was on the ground, I would look like just another clump of flowers to him if he glanced my way.

I looked up in time to see him drop to the patio, and I congratulated myself on being all but invisible to him from that lower angle. Then he got to his feet and headed directly toward me at a dead run.

All I could think of was that he had seen me from the window and was coming after me, and I turned suddenly cold with fear. Now, I know that in our macho society a lot of people pretend to like fighting. Hell, some of them may not even be pretending. But I'm not one of them. Like all schoolboys, I had been in my share of scuffles, and I had even gotten into one particularly stupid fight over a girl while I was in college. From these altercations I had learned two things: that fighting hurts, and that it hurts even more as you get older. If that alone had not dissuaded me from becoming a fighter, there was also the obvious fact that fighting never proved anything except who was the better fighter, which was seldom the point of contention. Of course, that was little comfort to me as I lay there beside the flower bed, watching the man run toward me with every apparent intention of doing me great bodily harm—or worse.

I have always contended that it is wisest to walk away from any fight that you can, but in this instance it was clear that I couldn't even *run* away from it, so I fell back on another of my axioms—when you can't avoid a fight, do your damnedest to win it. Accordingly, I gathered my legs beneath me as the man quickly closed the distance between us, and when he was only a few yards off, still travelling at full tilt, I launched myself at him, aiming for his middle with my right shoulder.

My attack seemed to take him by surprise, and only at the last moment did he make any effort to avoid it. But by then it was too late. His outstretched hands did little to soften the impact, and we smashed together with a dull, sickening thud. His momentum was too great to be halted completely by my charge, and he rolled over me onto the pathway, where he lay gasping for breath. My only damage was a slightly strained shoulder and a scratch beneath my left eye where one of his fingernails had grazed my face.

Lying there like a beached fish, the man no longer seemed much of a threat to me. It occurred to me, however, that he might be armed, so when I got to my feet I approached him cautiously, hoping that I could move quickly enough if he pulled a knife or a gun.

Finally catching his breath, the man looked up at me, and in the moonlight we recognized each other instantly.

"Goddamn it, John," Ben Latta croaked in a voice full of pain and anger, "what the bloody hell do you think you are doing?"

"*Me?*" I exclaimed indignantly as I helped him to his feet. "What the hell were *you* doing, charging down on me like that?"

He stood silently hunched over, gently rubbing his stomach while he breathed heavily. "You stupid bastard," he gasped out, "I didn't even know you were there until you jumped me."

"The hell you didn't," I responded with some heat. "You headed straight for me as soon as you hit the patio."

"I wasn't running at you, you idiot, I was running for the hedges in back."

I helped him over to the gazebo, where he settled gratefully down on the steps. When he was breathing more normally, he demanded that I explain my presence, and the tone of his voice made it clear that he intended to have an answer.

I stammered out an embarrassed explanation of how I had decided on my way home from class to have a look at the mansion, and that once I arrived I decided that a quick stroll around the grounds couldn't do any harm. "And when I saw you up there in the window I thought . . . . Well, I'm not sure now just what I thought, except that something was wrong. So I hid over there, and when you came stomping straight down my throat I tackled you in self-defense. Or, at least, I thought it was self-defense."

He didn't say anything for a moment, and in the moonlight I could see that he was thinking. Then he spoke: "I don't think I got around to asking this morning, John, but where were *you* around midnight last night?"

I felt a chill, and it was a moment before I answered. "I was at home. Alone. But you can't seriously think that I had anything to do with Marian's death. I know that it looks funny for me to be wandering around this place in the middle of the night, but what I told you is the truth: I only came because I was curious.

"Hell's bells, Ben," I continued, becoming quite alarmed at the possibility of being considered a suspect, "I thought you were convinced that Harrison was guilty—"

"Yeah, yeah," he interrupted me with a wave of his hand.

"Don't get excited." He looked at my face and then handed me a handkerchief from his jacket pocket. "Here," he said. "Your face is bleeding. Are you all right?"

I assured him that it was just a scratch. As I dabbed at it, an explanation of Ben's curious behavior occurred to me, and I asked, "You were acting out the part of Harrison's alleged intruder, weren't you?"

He looked at me for a long time without speaking, and when he did his voice was cold and formal: "Listen, John. This is a police investigation. It's not a parlor game in which all curious civilians are welcome to participate. You'll do well to keep your nose out of it and let us do our job. When we need your help, we'll ask for it. Until then, do yourself and me a favor and stay out of it."

He was right, and I knew it, but that didn't make it any easier for me to take. I didn't trust myself to speak, so I just turned and walked back up the pathway to the street, leaving him there with his aching stomach. I took my hurt feelings with me.

σ

The harsh ringing of the phone woke me from a deep sleep. As I rolled over toward the nightstand to answer it, I saw on the clock-radio's face that it was 5:43 a.m. "Hello?" I managed to croak.

"Johnny?" The voice that gratingly assaulted my sleep-sensitive ear was familiar, but I could not for the moment place it. "This is your Aunt Mildred. I tried several times to call you last night," she said, accusingly, "but you never answered. Your father is dead."

So like Aunt Mildred. Once when I was eleven years old, my best friend in the world, a jet-black cocker spaniel named Inky, was run over by a car while I was at school. The first thing Aunt Mildred said when I came through the front door was, "Your dog is dead. Go bury him." No cushioning of the blow. No offer of solace. I was never very fond of my Aunt Mildred.

Her announcement awoke me instantly, and I took stock of my emotions as she told me that my father had a massive heart attack at his shop the day before and expired in the hospital early last evening.

I was surprised, and a bit uncomfortable, to discover that I felt no gut-wrenching anguish at the news of my father's death.

He was dead, and that was that. Perhaps if we had been closer I would have felt more, but we had been at odds almost since I had begun to talk. Even so, a kaleidoscope of memories suddenly burst into my mind. But there was a peculiar remoteness to them, somewhat akin to a description of a meal someone else had eaten.

Aunt Mildred's abrasive voice brought me back to the present. "Mr. Shockley Smith himself is handling the arrangements," she was saying, "so all you have to do is show up for the funeral, which is tomorrow."

I didn't say anything. Funerals are hold-overs from man's barbarous past. They do no good whatever for the dead, and they only accentuate and prolong the grief of the living. I hated funerals, and I wanted to say I wasn't coming, but I knew that if I did she would badger me until I gave in. I could have hung up on her, but she would only have called back. Besides, my father was her brother, and, though I knew from my own experiences that she had all the sensitivity of an anesthetized rhinoceros, she was probably feeling something down under her thick skin, and my absence from the funeral could only add to her hurt.

At last I said, "I'll be there. Tell me what I need to know."

I called Dean Nathan's office as soon as I got to school. He was out, so I asked his secretary to tell him that I needed the rest of the week off. It being Thursday, I had no classes, and I left instructions at the department office for notices to be posted in my classrooms cancelling classes Friday. I had no trouble getting a seat on a flight that left at noon.

I thought about my father intermittently throughout the morning. Most of the time I was able to override those thoughts with whatever task was immediately at hand, but they were never far from the surface, and once, when I was asking Marge if she would be able to type up and run off an exam in time for my nine-o'clock class Monday, I completely lost the thread of what I was saying when my mind was suddenly filled with an image of my father's face. The bushy eyebrows, hooked nose, and thin-lipped mouth—all features which I had inherited in a slightly moderated form—were clear as a photograph, as was the stern look of disapproval that I remembered so well.

Plane connections to Everston were bad, and it took six

hours—half of them spent in terminals waiting for connecting flights—to get there. When the plane dipped its left wing-tip to turn into the final approach, it was already nearly dusk. Long shadows crept across the landscape below, making it difficult to pick out familiar landmarks. The courthouse and the surrounding business district were easy enough to find, and the high school was obvious, standing there isolated on its hill. But for the rest, I had difficulty meshing the ground-level memories of my youth with my aerial perspective.

The nearly obsolete craft belonging to the tiny regional airline which provided the only service to Everston touched down in a series of squeal-accompanied bounces and taxied to an abrupt halt before the single-storied cinderblock terminal.

Nearly a year had passed since my last visit, and a year can be a long or a short time, depending on your perspective. On this occasion it seemed very long indeed. The plane's sole stewardess finally managed to wrestle the door open, and two other passengers and I got to our feet, stretching our stiff muscles. As I stood there, not bothering to hide a yawn, a uniformed man pushed out a wheeled stairway. The stewardess bid us a good evening with a practiced, meaningless smile.

As I stepped out and breathed deeply to get rid of the close air of the plane, the sensation produced by that first lungful of fresh air was like an electrical shock. The grass along the runway had just been cut, and the warm, humid air was laden with the rich smell of newly mown grass. The scent unlocked a closet full of memories, and they came tumbling out as I descended to the ground. All at once I could see events from my past as vividly as though they were on film. Myself as a young boy, struggling desperately to push the old mower quickly around the yard so that I could join my friends in a nearby woods where we were building a fort. Myself as an adolescent, lying beneath the hedges on a pile of grass clippings with Claudette Bracken, the girl-next-door whose early blossoming bosom was the talk of the junior-high locker room. Myself and my father in a rare companionable moment, sitting beneath the pecan tree in the back yard, sipping lemonade as we discussed my impending departure for college.

I was caught up in this last memory and did not immediately recognize the man who stepped out to intercept me as I entered the terminal. I had not told Aunt Mildred when I would be arriving, and I planned to catch a cab to Everston's lone hotel, the Old South, which had stood for ages on Main Street overlooking the courthouse. Though I had lived my first eighteen years in this town, those years seemed to belong to another person's life. I had changed enormously since then, casting off a host of small-town prejudices in favor of more cosmopolitan beliefs which I told myself (not always convincingly) were more in keeping with the realities of the present. My visits home had quickly dwindled in number and duration. As an undergraduate I came home not more than twice during any semester, and by the time I received my B.A. the visits had bottomed out at about one a year. While I was in graduate school, my father and I kept in touch through long, disputatious, and often acrimonious letters which consumed great amounts of his time as well as mine and only succeeded in driving us further and further apart. A veteran of World War II, he considered himself a patriot; for my part, I was inclined to regard his love-it-or-leave-it attitude as unthinking at best and hypocritical at worst. He in turn regarded my opposition to the war in Viet Nam as un-American, if not—though he never said it—cowardly and treasonous.

I had been lucky where the war was concerned. My student deferments kept me out of the conflict, and I didn't have to flee to Canada, as I was fully prepared to do rather than participate in what I regarded as a grossly immoral enterprise. World War II being as close to a moral war as mankind is ever likely to come, my father was simply and honestly unable to understand my unwillingness to serve my country as he had served his. He had grown up at a time when patriotism was very much the norm, when the country's actions and motives were never questioned. Times had changed but his perceptions had not, and he demanded that I be loyal to something which no longer existed. And I, with the arrogance of youth, took more pleasure from scoring easy, cheap shots on the illogic of his position than I did from trying to explain to him the reasons for my own beliefs.

Thinking of this, I nearly bumped into the man before I noticed he was there. When he spoke my name I looked at him, taking in his thick blond hair, light blue eyes, and large, regular white teeth, without putting them all together at first.

"John," he repeated. "I'm your cousin Jeff. Mother asked me to meet your plane and give you a lift to town." I recognized him then. The hair, the eyes, and the teeth had all come from Aunt Mildred.

A large and handsome woman, my father's sister had doggedly held on to her maidenhood until I was in junior high school. From my point of view as a browbeaten nephew, I didn't think it could have been all that difficult for her to do, but apparently she had an entirely different effect on the adult men in her acquaintance, as she was never short of suitors. At the ripe age of thirty-five she finally gave in to the implorings of George Bell, our long-widowed high school biology teacher, and they were married when I was fourteen years old. Though she no longer lived in our house, she continued to boss my life as best she could from her new home several blocks away, even after her son Jeff was born almost a year to the day after her marriage.

I saw Jeff a good bit until I graduated from high school, although, since he was still a small child when I left, I didn't pay him much attention. I had seen him off and on when I returned for brief visits, but the last time he was a skinny, gangling, pimple-faced kid, quite different from the well-built, handsome young man who now stood before me. I realized with a shock that he must be in college by now, and I felt a bit uncomfortable with the realization that time marches on rather faster than we usually wish.

"Hi, Jeff," I said, extending my hand. "You've changed a lot."

He grinned and gave my hand a firm shake. "It's been five years, John; a person changes a lot between fourteen and nineteen." He looked at my carry-on bag and asked, "Is that all your luggage? Good. The car's right outside."

He led the way out the swinging glass doors to the small adjacent parking lot. The car was an old Mustang convertible which was obviously being restored. Extensive body work had already been done; bruise-colored primer covered more than half of the car's exterior. I tossed my bag in the back and climbed in.

As Jeff maneuvered out of the parking lot—driving quite reasonably, I was pleased to note—he said, "Mom said to tell you she's got a bed fixed for you at home."

I had feared this all along. The truth was that I didn't want to be around people any more than I had to. It wasn't that I wanted to be alone with my grief; it was simply that I didn't wish to have to play the role of a grief-stricken son. I felt a numbness, a slight hollowness which had not gone away since Aunt Mildred's call, but it did not stop me from behaving in a perfectly normal fashion. I still smiled when I saw children at play and laughed when I heard a witty remark, and I didn't think that such an absence of overt grief would sit very well with my conventional aunt and her friends. I couldn't grieve the way they would expect me to, and I wasn't about to make everyone uncomfortable by my non-grieving presence.

"That's very kind of your mother, Jeff," I replied, "but I've got a room reserved at the Old South." That was true. The last time the Old South had been full was in the early fifties, when Eisenhower, still just a general, came to town for a day of political stumping in his first campaign for the presidency, and I knew that there was no need whatever for me to make reservations in advance. But having them gave me the only thin excuse I could think of to decline an invitation to stay with relatives, so I had made the phone call and told the surprised clerk to hold a room for me for the night.

Jeff didn't make a big issue of my refusal, so I guessed that Aunt Mildred hadn't been all that enthusiastic about having me as a house guest after all.

We drove quickly into town, the open top making conversation at normal tones quite impossible. Instead of stopping in the street outside the hotel to let me out, Jeff pulled into a parking place not far from the entrance and killed the engine. He sat there, making no move to get out, and I guessed that he wanted me to ask him to come in with me. The bright grin that split his face when I did confirmed my guess, and he held the door open for me as we entered the dark lobby of the Old South Hotel.

The hotel was typical of the kind of establishment that could be found in virtually every city and town in the South before the advent of motels. It was three stories high and took up half of one of the four blocks facing the courthouse. It was hard to imagine its rooms ever being full.

I walked over to the registration counter, behind which stood a tall warren of letter slots, most of them empty except for pairs of keys. To the left, almost out of sight behind a partition, stood an ancient telegraph machine. A small plaque on the wall indicated that Western Union was still putting the old machine to work on the rare occasion that anyone had an anachronistic urge to send a telegram.

A huge ceiling fan revolved slowly, maintaining a slight breeze in the dark lobby, all the windows of which were open to the outside. I tapped lightly on the bell on the counter. An elderly woman came out from behind the partition and smiled sweetly at me.

"You have a reservation for John Forest, I believe?" I asked.

She nodded cheerfully and said, "Yes, sir, Mr. Forest. We've given you the Governor's Suite."

Jeff gave me a slow wink as the woman turned the registration book around for me to sign.

"It's just at the head of the stairs, Mr. Forest," she said, handing me a large key attached to an even larger plastic board on which the number 201 was imprinted in white. "You'll have to tote your bag yourself, I'm afraid. Jimmy's been out with the rheumatism since last fall."

"I can manage just fine, thank you ma'am. Is there room service?"

"Yes, sir. What would you like?"

"A couple of cold beers would go right nice on a warm evening like this," I said, slipping easily into the speech patterns of my youth.

Her smile was even warmer as she replied, "I'll send them right up." The familiar sounds had reassured her that I wasn't, after all, a complete foreigner.

I thanked her, and Jeff and I climbed the long flight to the second floor. A chain across the stairs to the third floor indicated that the top story was not being used. The Governor's Suite turned out to be two identical small rooms with an open connecting door and a single bath between them. Faded wallpaper decorated each room, the narrow beds stood high off the floor, and the dressers appeared to be at least as old as the hotel. The bathroom fixtures also seemed to be original equipment; the tub was even supported by four sturdy claws. A huge, ancient, black-and-white television with a tiny screen crouched in the corner of one room next to the window. The spreads on both beds were faded, but clean. Indeed, the entire "suite" was spotless. It wasn't Holiday Inn-modern, but then neither was the price; I had to look twice at the rate card on the back of the door before I could accept the fact that the single rate was only twelve dollars a day.

I motioned Jeff to the room's sole chair and plopped myself

down on the bed, using the pillows to make a back rest against the headboard. I had just gotten comfortable when there was a knock on the door.

An elderly black man in a dusty old uniform which may once have been purple brought in a tray with two glasses and two sweating bottles of beer and placed it on the dresser. The chit was for a dollar-fifty, so I gave him three dollars and then had to listen to his profuse thanks all the way to the door.

Jeff obviously wanted to talk but was having trouble getting started, so I asked him about the funeral arrangements. He said that there would be a service at the church at eleven, to be followed by a burial service at the cemetery at twelve, after which family and friends were to gather at Aunt Mildred's house for a buffet lunch. I refrained from expressing any opinion on this arrangement, but something must have shown on my face because he smiled and said, "Mother says that funerals are a way of showing respect for the dead."

"Yeah?" I replied. "And what do you say?"

He replied with some heat, which seemed to be directed at me, "I say that the time to show people respect is when they are alive, not after they are dead." He paused, and then he added in a softer voice, "He really loved you, you know."

For the next half hour Jeff told me a great deal about the stranger who was my father, things that I had not known or understood. Then he took his leave to change from jeans into slacks and a coat before taking me by the funeral home. He said he'd return about nine. Before he left he shook my hand and said, "It's good to see you again, even under these circumstances."

After he was gone I spent a long time trying to think of one good reason why I should have stayed away so long. I couldn't do it.

7

I tried watching some television to while away the time until Jeff's return. Two minutes after I turned on the antique set, during which the aged tubes were presumably stretching their muscles to get the kinks out, a picture gradually formed on the tiny screen, blossoming slowly from the center outward. I flipped the channel selector completely around twice, but the most watchable program was one of those idiot game shows in which the contestants comport themselves like a squealing herd of pigs. There was a certain quaint charm about the nearly round, black-and-white tube, but the show was so ridiculous that I soon got up and turned it off in disgust.

I lay down on the bed and tried to keep my mind off the sensitive matters Jeff had brought up by thinking of something else. The only topic with any hope of occupying my attention was Marian's murder, so I turned my mind to it as fully as I could.

I had, in fact, had little time to puzzle over it since my run-in with Ben the night before. I knew that it was none of my business and that I had come perilously close to getting myself into serious trouble by nosing about, but there was no reason why I couldn't just think about it.

So think I did, right up until Jeff knocked on the door promptly at nine. I thought about Harrison and how unlikely it seemed to me that he would murder Marian, even though Ben appeared to be quite convinced that he had—well, perhaps not *entirely* convinced, or why would he have bothered to check out Harrison's intruder story so completely? I thought about Marian, and I wondered what she could have done to make Harrison, or somebody else, kill her. And when I got nowhere thinking about Harrison and Marian, I thought about other people who might have wanted to kill her—about Kate Roeder, Kenneth Phillips. That was even less satisfactory.

By the time Jeff arrived, I had practically thought myself into a stupor. I didn't learn anything by it, but at least it had kept my mind occupied.

Smith's Funeral Home was an imposing structure, as most of those establishments usually are. I have never really understood why that should be: why funeral homes—what a ghastly misuse of the word "home"—should almost invariably be huge mansions or towering edifices of concrete and glass, rather than more modest buildings. Possibly there is some vague intent to imply the existence of a kind of dignity in death—though death is not generally all that dignified—but more likely the size and ostentation are there as justification for the astronomically high bills with which the bereaved are presented as soon as the last clod has been tapped smooth on the grave mound.

Whatever the reason, Smith's Funeral Home vigorously kept up the tradition. It was a huge, square building, several hundred feet on a side, topped by a pyramidal roof that would have done one of the lesser pharoahs proud. The interior of the building, at least the part of it that laymen were allowed to see, was decorated with all the charm, restraint, and good taste that one might expect to find in a brothel that catered to the nouveau riche.

On an easel in the lobby stood a somber, black-draped sign with two columns of names. On the left were family names, and on the right were the names of rooms. "Forest—Serenity Room" was third from the top. An unctuous young man in a black suit and tie glided into the lobby a few seconds after we entered and, in answer to my query, informed us that the

Serenity Room was the third door down the corridor to the right. We moved off without thanking him.

Soft voices floated into the hallway from the first two doors, borne on a tide of flower scents that almost made me gag with their sweetness. The Serenity Room proved to be a large chamber with upholstered benches along the walls and several stuffed chairs arranged in the corners. The room was half filled with people, but the first thing that caught the eye was the large open casket near the door.

Ever since I had been coerced into serving as a pallbearer for a young acquaintance who had committed suicide when I was fifteen, I had been unalterably opposed to funerals. I could still hear the boy's mother's screams in my mind's ear, rising throughout the service to drown out the minister's voice. Until then I hadn't really given funerals much thought, but I thought about them quite intensely as I sat there on the hard pew and listened to her wail. Her son had been dead for three days, and her grief had been kept hyped up for all that time. She couldn't begin to cope with her loss until she had gone through the ritual.

Funerals don't benefit the dead—they are out of it. And, despite all the talk I had heard about their necessity for the psychological well-being of the survivors, I remained convinced that they don't benefit the living, either. The time to start dealing with the death of a loved one is the moment that person dies, not several days later when the barbaric funeral rites have been performed. My young friend's mother was permanently scarred by the wait; her psychological well-being was not promoted by her son's funeral, and mine wasn't being promoted by my father's.

I stepped across to the coffin and looked down on my father's remains. They looked about as much like he had looked in life as wax busts in Madame Tussaud's resemble the personages they are intended to portray. His skin had a waxy, gray look, except where the mortician had been too liberal with the rouge and had given his cheeks a healthy red glow. The wrinkles that had been as much a part of my father's face as his large hooked nose were all gone, smoothed out by a few cosmetic touches. And his lips were arranged in a sanctimonious smile that would never have crossed them when he was alive. I could feel the rage boiling up inside me as I stood there.

Then, just as I was about to explode, I felt a persistent nudge in my right side and was shouldered out of the way by a spry old woman who must have been in her eighties. She was small enough that she had to stand close to the coffin in order to see in, and she muttered under her breath as she craned her scrawny neck this way and that to take it all in. Then she stood back, looked up at me, and said with a toothless smile, "Mighty nice lookin' feller, ain't he?" before tottering out, presumably to pass judgement on the temporary residents of the "Eternity Room," the "Blissful Sleep Room," and the other similarly named rooms of Smith's Funeral Home.

The absurdity of the event dispelled most of my rage, and I was able to turn back to the crowd with at least a trace of civility. Most of the people were friends of my father, people I had only distantly known as a child knows his father's acquaintances, but there was a scattering of relatives as well, mostly cousins on my mother's side. Having put in my appearance as required, I made the rounds, speaking as familiarly as I could to those I remembered and pretending to recognize those whom I had in fact forgotten. Jeff was a big help with that, introducing people in such a way that I knew whether I should have remembered them even if I didn't. I got away as soon as I could, but it was still nearly eleven when I got back to the hotel.

I was exhausted and wanted nothing more than to fall into bed, but I felt grimy after the day's events and I knew I'd never get to sleep if I didn't bathe first. As it happened, I nearly fell asleep in the tub—the Old South didn't run to showers—and when I finally got to bed I was out in two minutes.

For the most part I slept soundly, but at one point during the night I had a disquieting dream in which my father and I exchanged roles. We had retained our appearances except for our sizes. Though a middle-aged man, my father was less than five feet tall in the dream, and I, though less than twelve years old, towered over him by more than a foot. In the dream I was the father and he the son, and I was sorely disappointed in him. Instead of staying in the house and reading the books I had selected for him, he had sneaked off and gone fishing. I would have to come up with a punishment suitable to his transgression. In the meantime, I wasn't speaking to him.

I woke up at that point and was surprised to find tears in my eyes. I drifted back to sleep before I could decide which of us I was crying for.

I was awakened again before the night was out, but not by another dream. The Old South Hotel had been built in more innocent times, and the locks on its doors were the simple kind that can be opened with any dimestore skeleton key. Also, because of their considerable age, they tended to squeak and squeal when they were opened. At least mine did, and it was the noise of the lock mechanism being turned that first began to rouse me from my sleep.

I was exhausted, both physically and emotionally, and after my nightmare I had fallen into a deep, dark, oblivious slumber. When the squeaking came my mind tried to fit it into a dream, but there was no dream handy, so the noise lay there as incongruous as a live fish in the center of an empty basketball court. I tried to ignore it, not wanting to stir from the dark, safe womb of sleep, but it and other tiny sounds continued to peck away at my slumber, keeping me from slipping back into restful unconsciousness.

The noises roiled the surface of my mind, and fragments of thought rose and fell in a patternless jumble — my father's face swam to the surface, smiling as he had when, at the age of five, I presented him with a primitive pipe I had made from an acorn and the tip of an old cane fishing pole; that image dissolved and was replaced by his face as I had seen it only a few hours earlier, wearing the alien smile put there by a careless or unfeeling mortician; then that image gave way to Marian James-Tyrell's face as I remembered it, her arch, self-satisfied smile confidently in place; then it was transformed by a horrified, open-eyed grimace, as Marian must have looked when her killer pressed the life out of her with a pillow.

It was at this point that the spare pillow on my bed was stealthily raised, and I fought my way up to full consciousness, scrambling frantically to the opposite side of the bed, all the while emitting a noise which was an embarrassing combination of wheeze and shriek.

The moment I began to move, the intruder dropped the pillow and bolted for the door, knocking aside the chair in his haste. I went off the far side of the bed at the same time that he opened the door, so I caught nothing more than a blurred glimpse of some form before I fell the considerable distance to the threadbare carpet. The door slammed behind him, and I lay there for several seconds, listening to my racing heart and feeling the sweat pop out all over my body.

Finally, I got shakily to my feet and cautiously opened the door to the hall. No one was in the dimly lit corridor, but the barely perceptible swaying of the chain across the stairway to the third floor suggested that my intruder had gone up instead of down. I dismissed any thought of following him. He had probably already made good his escape, and if he hadn't I'd be at a distinct disadvantage stumbling around in the dark trying to find him.

I closed the door, locked it again (for all that was worth), then dragged the chair over and wedged it beneath the handle. I did the same in the adjoining room, and then I sat down on my bed to think things over. My first thought was to call the police, but I realized that was unlikely to accomplish anything except keep me from getting any more sleep that night. Everston's police force was no worse than any other small-town constabulary, but it wasn't any better, either, and it was most unlikely that anything would come of an investigation.

What, after all, had happened? Someone had broken into my hotel room and had run off when I awakened. It wasn't exactly the crime of the century. I got up off the bed and looked around the room. I had emptied my pockets carelessly on the dresser, so I couldn't tell if anything had been disturbed. My wallet was where I had put it—in one of my shoes beneath the bed—and its contents were undisturbed. My one piece of luggage looked a bit mussed, but I couldn't be certain that I hadn't left it like that myself.

The only thing I could say for sure was that, if the intruder had been looking for something to steal, he had gone away empty-handed.

But if he wasn't after something to steal, why on earth had he come into my room? I puzzled over that for a few minutes before an extremely unpleasant possibility occurred to me. Actually, I suppose it had been lurking about in the recesses of my mind ever since the moment the intruder's actions brought me back to total consciousness, but it seemed so fantastic that I couldn't at first credit it.

I shut my eyes for a moment and strained to recall the details of my awakening. The progression of faces in my sleep was still vivid, especially Marian's horrified, eye-bulging grimace, which flashed into my mind the moment the intruder lifted the spare pillow from my bed. It was, of course, entirely possible that he was merely looking beneath the pillow to see if I had hidden my wallet there. But it was also possible—not very likely, perhaps, but certainly possible—that he had had another reason for lifting it.

"Ridiculous," I said aloud with a snort and a shake of my head. But I wasn't entirely convinced. Perhaps it was the atmosphere—being alone in an ancient hotel in a town that had become a strange place to me, being there to attend my father's funeral—on top of the depressing evening at the funeral home. Probably it was a combination of all those things which put me in a morbid frame of mind. Still, I could not help but wonder whether my intruder was not the same person who had stolen into Marian's bedroom and smothered the life out of her.

But the police seemed certain that Harrison had done it, and I had no reason to think that he was at liberty. Besides, Everston was hundreds of miles from Brookleigh, and it was ludicrous to think that Marian's killer, even if he were still at large, would travel all that distance to snuff me out in the same manner. Besides, who knew that I'd be here, anyway?

That question no sooner occurred to me than I realized that a great many people, both in Brookleigh and in Everston, would know where I was. It is as difficult to keep secrets on a college campus as in a small town, particularly when there is no reason for them to be kept secret in the first place.

But why on earth would someone want to kill me at all, much less in the same manner in which Marian had been killed? There was no connection between us, no possible linking which might have given a killer one motive for wanting both of us dead. It was, I finally agreed with myself, ridiculous. I had just been the victim of an inept would-be hotel burglar, and I was blowing it all out of proportion, allowing the morbid thoughts that filled my mind to conjure up menaces where none existed.

I finally decided I was just wasting good sleeping time by worrying about it, so I got back into bed and tried to go back to sleep. But it was a long time—a time in which my mind was filled with thoughts of death and pillows and murder—before I drifted off again.

For some bizarre reason known best to my Aunt Mildred, she had arranged to have the funeral service held in a tiny old wooden church fifteen miles on the other side of town from the cemetery. Jeff said that he thought my father and Aunt Mildred had attended church there as children. I didn't press the matter because, frankly, at that moment I just didn't care. All I wanted to do was get all the rituals completed, and I had learned as a child that, where Aunt Mildred was concerned, demanding explanations for why something had to be done her way only delayed the inevitable.

The small parking lot at the church, which was on a narrow country lane in the middle of nowhere, was filled to overflowing. I was surprised to see so many people turn out to pay their last respects to my father. The sermon was mercifully brief, but the confusion of organizing the funeral procession produced long delays. When it finally got under way, the trip to the cemetery was uneventful. More words had to be spoken over the casket at the graveside before convention finally allowed my father to be lowered into the ground.

That done at last, the entire cortege, minus the hearse and the limousines which were relinquished back to their caretakers, drove to Aunt Mildred's, where a lavish spread had been prepared. The buffet was a break from the somber atmosphere of the earlier proceedings. The guests laughed and smiled when conversing with each other, and many of them came up to me with expressions of sympathy and words of warm, sincere praise for my father that went beyond the standard he-was-a-fine-man platitudes which are said about virtually anyone who dies, from the best of us to the worst.

I was rather surprised at the warmth with which my father had apparently been regarded. I knew that he had been an honest, hard-working, moral man, but the principal personality characteristics that I remembered were inflexibility and aloofness. As I listened to the remarks of people who clearly knew him better than I had, I began at last to realize how truly we had been strangers to each other.

He had evidently changed considerably since I had left home—or else my perception of him had been distorted all along. The words of his friends revealed a kind, tolerant, understanding man, generous with both his time and his money. I knew that he had been a marvelously skilled cabinet maker, a rare thing in these days of assembly lines and mass production, and that he had made a very comfortable living practicing his craft for those who could afford to pay for quality workmanship.

62

But I was unaware, until a rotund, clerical-collared gentleman whose name I did not catch told me, as he munched his way through a plate of celery and carrot sticks, that my father had routinely plied his skills after hours at various worthy locations around town, at no charge whatever. "Your father was a great help to us when we were converting the old Haines home into a youth shelter," he said. "I don't think we could have managed without him." And a tall man with an upright, military bearing, who introduced himself simply as "Haley," told me that my father had been a great help to him in his work with youth groups, giving them lessons in handicrafts and accompanying them on camping trips.

Coupled with what Jeff had told me, these new revelations painted a picture of my father completely different from the one I had held for years, and the uncomfortable feelings I had experienced the night before rushed back in full force. Again, my reaction was a compound of guilt and resentment. Guilt that I had so isolated myself from my father that I was unaware of what he had become, and resentment that he had kept this side of his personality from me.

Or had I simply not given him the opportunity to display it? I thought back over the pattern into which our rare meetings had fallen over the years. The first few moments of meeting, the pleasure of seeing each other again after a lapse of time, were always the best for both of us. The smiles were genuine, the handclasps firm and sincere. We always tried to keep our conversation on neutral subjects—how things were going at his shop and my school, what kind of a flight I had had, how his health was holding up—but, inevitably, one of us would make a remark on a matter of substance and a stiffness would instantly set in. We had gotten to the point where we could avoid actual arguments, but the strain was severe on both of us. Meetings of an hour or so were about all that either of us could tolerate.

I was one of the first to leave Aunt Mildred's, as I had to catch a four-o'clock flight back to Brookleigh. My good-bye to Aunt Mildred was the longest conversation we had all day. We had kissed and spoken at the funeral home the night before, but it was all perfunctory. And we had little more to say as I prepared to leave. We had never been the least bit fond of each other, and that would never change. I thanked her for taking care of things in Everston, and she said that Harley Wilson, my father's lawyer, would be in touch with me about the will. I gave her another peck on the cheek before leaving.

Jeff drove me to the airport in his Mustang, and on the way I just leaned back in the seat and closed my eyes. I had a lot to think about after this trip, and it was going to be a long time before I got it all sorted out in my mind.

8

It was late Saturday morning before I awoke. The flight back to Brookleigh had been long, boring, and uneventful. I had come straight home from the airport to find, on the third-floor landing outside the door of my apartment, a fifth of Beefeater gin with a plain card scotch-taped to the neck. The card contained the word "Sorry" and the name Herbie. I unlocked my door, dropped my bag just inside, and made for the kitchen at the rear. There was half a bottle of nearly flat tonic water in the refrigerator, and I used it and Herbie's gin to make a tall drink which I put away while standing in the kitchen.

Herbert T. Palmer was my landlord. I had met him when I rented the apartment, and I had had some trouble figuring him out at first. He owned Palmer's Funeral Home and the three-storied building in which the business and my apartment were housed, but Herbie appeared to be anything but a mortician. A pudgy little man of about forty-five, his round face emitted a steady beam of happiness. His eyes twinkled constantly, and his mouth always looked as though it was about to break into a big smile—which it usually was. After I got to know him, I learned that in his case appearances were not deceiving—he was exactly the cheerful fellow he seemed to be.

One day my curiosity got the best of me, and I said to him, "Why on earth did you ever decide to become a mortician?"

"I didn't," he replied with his infectious laugh. "That is, I'm not a mortician. I'm a flower child, actually. I mean, that's what I set out to be. And then my great-uncle Horatio Palmer, who founded this establishment, up and died and confronted me with a true dilemma."

I knew Herbie well enough by then to realize that he was about to launch into one of his unfailingly entertaining stories, so I settled back and relaxed.

"Uncle Horatio, you see, was a lifelong bachelor whose only interests were in burying people and making money. I was his only living relative, and when I graduated from high school he offered to take me into his business as a junior partner, to take over when he finally died. I turned him down flat, loftily telling him that I held him and his materialistic world in the deepest contempt and I wanted no part of his ghoulish business."

Herbie winked at me and said, "I had a small annuity from my parents, you understand, and I could afford to make grand gestures. After that, I coasted through college before setting out to become a beatnik, as we called ourselves back then. We sat around in coffee houses, sang or recited long, boring, doom-laden lyrics to each other, and pretended that we were the only sighted people in a blind world. Ah, Johnny boy, it was great—if you were into self-indulgent hypocrisy.

"Of course, Uncle Horatio saw through it all, and when the old bastard died he left his entire estate to me, on the condition that I come back and run the business for ten years. If I declined the inheritance, or if I failed to stick it out for a full decade, his entire estate was to be used to establish a commune for flower children." Herbie laughed uproariously at this.

"He knew damned well that I wouldn't let a bunch of people like those I was associating with get hold of all his money, so I came back, traded in my long beard and beads for a black suit and a short haircut, and settled down to become a gentleman mortician. Actually, though, the first thing I did was hire a capable mortician to run the place, and then I turned it all over to him. That was twenty years ago. I handle the strictly business end of things, but I steer clear of the embalming and funeral arrangements and the rest of that stuff. To tell the truth," he said with a shudder, "it gives me the creeps."

Sometimes, when Herbie had been working late in his second

floor office, he would pop up to my apartment for a couple of beers or something stronger before going home to his highly respectable wife and their two stuffy young teen-aged daughters. "Take after their mother, the girls do," he once told me ruefully. "Not an unconventional bone in their scrawny little bodies." But it was evidently a loving family, and Herbie never had any complaints. He was also a fair-to-middling chess player, and we spent a couple of evenings each month battling it out over a chess board. We were pretty evenly matched, so it was usually a good contest.

Herbie was good for me. When I was around him I always found myself relaxing. He had an endless supply of stories about his disreputable past, most of which I suspected him of making up out of whole cloth, and his conversation was invariably enjoyable. And he was a good listener as well. I numbered him as one of my closest friends. If I needed someone to talk to, I knew that Herbie would be happy to listen. But he was always careful not to intrude, and he knew that I would call him if I needed him. Which was why he left it at a bottle of Beefeater and a one-word note.

I had another stiff drink before going to bed Friday night, which accounted for my sleeping late the next morning. I finally dragged myself out of bed, washed up, and slipped into my weekend uniform of jeans, sneakers, and T-shirt before running downstairs to collect the mail and the newspapers, which I had neglected to pick up the night before. The mail was mostly bills and circulars, so I looked through the newspapers which had accumulated in the box since my departure Thursday, taking alternating sips from the cup of steaming coffee and the large, cold glass of grapefruit juice which passed for breakfast around my bachelor establishment.

The biggest news, of course, was Marian's murder. I took only the local afternoon paper, and I usually didn't bother to read it, but Wednesday's *Ledger* had carried a front-page story with Corinne's by-line under the head: BEAUTIFUL COLLEGE PROFESSOR MURDERED! ("Don't blame me for the headlines," she had told me more than once, "because I don't write them; my editor does.") Since, as I knew from better times with Corinne, the paper's deadline was ten in the morning, her story had contained even less than I had gotten from Ben Latta, except for some hurriedly gathered comments from neighbors and members of the English department.

Now, over my second cup of coffee, I looked for the follow-up story in Thursday's paper. The headline—MURDER VICTIM'S SPOUSE RELEASED—caught my attention immediately, and I read with close attention. I was surprised to learn that the news of Harrison's release was almost a day old before Thursday's paper hit the streets. (One of Corinne's most frequent complaints about working on an afternoon paper was that, with a mid-morning deadline, reporters were often reduced to writing about yesterday's news.)

According to Corinne's story, the police had released Harrison from custody Wednesday afternoon without giving any reason. That explained why Ben had been checking out the intruder story Wednesday night—his prime suspect had been sprung, and he still had a murderer to catch. I could understand a little better, now, why he had been annoyed with my presence on the grounds of the Tyrell estate, though I was still hurt that he hadn't bothered to tell me that Harrison had been released. But, considering the circumstances of our encounter, it wasn't hard to understand why he had been uncommunicative. My preoccupation with my father's death and the unwillingness of my colleagues to intrude upon my grief at the time explained why I hadn't heard anything about Harrison's release before I left for the funeral.

In her Thursday story, Corinne managed to give the impression, without actually saying so, that Harrison had been taken into custody as the likely murderer of his wife, but that the police had uncovered some evidence which removed him from suspicion, at least for the time being. Thinking back on what Ben had told me Wednesday morning, it seemed likely that the police had found some evidence at the Tyrell mansion to prove the existence of a prowler, but there was nothing in the article to suggest that this was the case. Indeed, although the article was several times longer than the one in Wednesday's paper, the only news in it was Harrison's release; the rest was just a rehash of what I had learned before I left.

A quick glance was all I needed to see that Friday's paper was no more informative. I finally tossed the paper aside and was rinsing out my cup and glass when the phone rang. It was Corinne. "I'm sorry about your father, John," she said in a voice almost as warm as it had been before our troubles. "I tried to get you at your office Thursday afternoon, and Mrs. Cominos told me you'd gone to attend his funeral. Is there anything I can do?"

She sounded as though she meant it, and for a moment I had a nearly overwhelming desire to be with her, to tell her some of the things that had been going through my head since my father's death. I started to ask her to come over, but at the last moment I caught myself. Instead, I thanked her for her concern and told her that I didn't need anything. That sounded rather harsh, so to soften it and to keep from putting her off altogether I asked her about the James-Tyrell case.

"Buy a newspaper," she said with some of her old spirit, proving that she hadn't interpreted what I had said as a rejection.

"I have," I replied, "but it doesn't tell me much. What are you holding out on your reading public?"

I asked the question more or less in jest, but Corinne's silence indicated that I had hit home. "You *are* holding out, aren't you? Come on, Corinne, what is it? Do you know what evidence the police have that caused them to let Harrison go?"

She knew, but she wasn't telling, and after badgering her a bit longer I finally gave it up.

"I'm sorry, John," she said. "I'd tell you if I could. I really would. But I'm under orders from the police themselves not to print it or tell anyone about it, and it would cost me at least my job if I said anything, even to you."

I told her that I understood, and we said good-bye, with her repeating her expressions of sympathy. After we hung up I thought for a few minutes about Corinne and me. That telephone conversation, and the one on Wednesday, had brought us closer together than I ever imagined we would be again, and I was still undecided whether it was a good thing or not.

But dwelling on that question was no better for my morale than thinking constantly about my father, so I decided to go over to the college and do some work to keep my mind occupied.

It was a bright sunshiny day, with just enough of a breeze blowing to keep it from becoming uncomfortably warm. Even so, I'm a brisk walker, and I was sweating lightly when I got to the campus. Brookleigh doesn't hold classes on Saturdays except during the summer, so the academic buildings are generally locked throughout the weekend. I used my key to get into the social science building, picked up my briefcase and a couple of fresh legal pads from my office, and then headed for the library.

I was, I thought wryly as I crossed the nearly deserted campus, hot on the trail of a murderer. Some months earlier, while reading through some early nineteenth-century newspapers for an article I was doing on Anglo-French diplomatic relations, I had come across a series of news stories about a fascinating murder which had just taken place in London. The newspapers gave it full coverage, complete with diagrams and drawings of the murder scene, and I had followed the reports through several days before reluctantly returning to the more prosaic task I had originally set out on. I had not, however, forgotten about the murder, and I had an idea that I might get an interesting article out of it if the later reports were half as interesting as the ones I had skimmed through. It was not the sort of thing that the stuffier journals would be interested in publishing, but one of the popular-history journals would gobble it up. And, unlike their more elevated brethren, the popular journals *paid* for articles.

The library stayed open through the weekend, and I was soon seated before a microfilm viewer, reading newspapers a century and a half old. I became so engrossed in the case that it was midafternoon before tired eyes and a distended bladder forced me to call it a day. I stopped off at the social science building to drop off my notes, and I was strolling back in the direction of Palmer's Funeral Home when I spotted a familiar figure coming toward me on the walk.

It was Harrison James, striding from his office to the faculty parking lot, where his red Porsche glowed in the afternoon sunlight. His handsome features, dominated by a trim beard he had grown during the previous winter, had a somber look, but there was nothing in the way his slight body moved to indicate that he had recently suffered a great loss. He seemed to be bearing up well.

Harrison and I were acquaintances only, not close friends, but the coincidence of his wife and my father dying only a few hours apart made me feel a degree of kinship with him, so it was with more than my usual amount of feeling that I commiserated with him over Marian's death. He had heard about my father as well and returned my expressions of sympathy, then we stood there for several uncomfortable moments with nothing further to say. More to break the silence than for any other reason, I brought up the subject of Marian's murder.

"Do the police have any leads, Harrison?" I asked.

"If they do, they're not confiding in me. In fact," he added with a humorless chuckle and a shake of his head which seemed to say that it was too incredible to believe, "they seemed for a time to think that *I* did it. But something happened to make them change their minds finally, and they had to let me go."

"Do you know what it was?" I asked. "The newspaper mentioned something about evidence, but it didn't say what it was."

"I don't know either," he said, shaking his head again, "but I'm awfully glad that they found it, whatever it was. I was beginning to think they were never going to let me out. I'd never been in jail before, of course, and it wasn't at all pleasant."

"I suppose not," I said, sympathetically. "Do you have any idea who the police suspect, or even, for that matter, if they have any suspects at all in mind?"

"Well, they asked me a lot of questions about Kate Roeder. And about Kenneth Phillips." He colored slightly at the second name and suddenly appeared to be in a hurry. Glancing at his watch, he said, "Well, I've got to be going, John. Drop by and have a drink some time."

"I'll do that," I replied as he hurried off. And I meant it. Harrison seemed to be a nice enough fellow, and he could use some support at this point in his life. Besides, I thought, I could use a few more friends myself. That thought surprised me, surfacing entirely on its own volition. I wondered briefly what my subconscious meant by it. I shrugged and walked back to the apartment.

That night my father was very much on my mind. I wasn't ready yet to think about what Jeff had told me at the Old South two nights before, but remembrances of my childhood kept breaking through the mental barriers I tried to erect. One particular memory, of the single occasion my father had taken me hunting, kept popping up in my mind with startling clarity.

My father had been a very opinionated man. He had a good mind, but it stayed closed most of the time. Once he latched onto an idea, it was his forever. I grew up a curious child, questioning everything I saw, and my father tried at first to impose his prejudices on me. Eventually, as I persisted in asking why even after he had told me what he thought I ought to believe, he began to have less and less to do with me. For my part, when my questions began to be greeted by grunts or, what was worse, silence from my father, and when my mother could only say, "I don't know, dear," I began to look elsewhere for the answers.

I found them, before long, in books. After that I ceased to bother my father with questions, but that did nothing to heal the breach between us, for my father regarded my bookish habits as unmanly. When I was in my early teens he decided to make an effort to reach me through the masculine arts of hunting and fishing. The fishing came first, and he spent several afternoons sitting at one end of a small boat, telling me the best spots to throw my line. As I am one of those rare individuals at whom fish can thumb their noses with absolute impunity, these trips were total failures. But they were nothing compared to our hunting outing the following fall.

I knew what my father was trying to do, and I genuinely appreciated it. Indeed, after years of neglect it warmed my heart greatly for him to take so much time and trouble with me. But I was, for all that, still a curious child, and it was that curiosity that put an end to this brief episode of father-son outdoor activity.

He woke me up quite early that brisk fall morning, and we were in place in a wooded area before the first rays of sunlight made their way through the trees. We were hunting squirrels, and my father positioned me near a tree which he knew from past experience was frequented by large numbers of those creatures.

"Keep still, son, and pretty soon you'll have a shot," he said, and with that he walked away to find a tree for himself. I heard him moving softly through the trees for a few minutes, then there was nothing but silence.

I waited, as quietly and as patiently as I could, while the black-on-black image of the woods around me was transformed into a picture of brightly lit fall colors, like an image emerging on a piece of exposed photographic paper. The coming of dawn caused hundreds of birds to burst into song, and the woods came alive with brisk, rustling noises. I watched very carefully the tree my father had pointed out, and from time to time I could see dark shapes scurrying about on its limbs. But they were always too far away and too indistinct; even if they were squirrels, of which I was not at all certain, I had not the slightest doubt that if I fired my rifle at them I would miss.

Though I was not particularly keen about shooting squirrels—I would rather have been playing baseball or swimming than sitting beneath a tree for hours in hopes of getting a shot at a tree-climbing rodent—I did want to please my father, and I didn't think he would be especially happy with my wasting ammunition without hitting anything. So I waited for a good shot to come along. And I waited. From time to time I heard my father shoot a hundred or so yards away, but, although I continued to scan my tree diligently, no clear shot presented itself to my untrained eye.

Before long I became bored with sitting there, waiting for some obliging squirrel to give me a shot. I began to cast my eye around my immediate vicinity, and I found much more there to hold my attention. A rough-scaled lizard sat patiently on a broken limb not a dozen feet from me. Its gray-brown coloration blended perfectly with the weathered bark, and I would not have noticed it at all had I not been looking in its direction when it lunged a few inches to gobble up an unwary insect. When I glanced back at it after looking away for a few minutes I thought at first that it had gone, but it was still there, all but invisible on its perch. I also spotted a sphinx-like toad and three energetic beetles before my attention was drawn to a large, flat rock a few feet away.

As any child can attest, rocks make excellent hiding places for numerous tiny creatures, and I was lying there on my belly, watching countless ants scurrying about trying to repair the damage I had done to their home by lifting off its roof, when my father spoke not ten feet away.

So intense was my concentration on the microscopic world I had disturbed, I had not heard him approach, and I don't know how long he had been standing there. It must have been a while, though, because the anger which my transgressions usually elicited from him had drained away, and what remained was weary resignation. All he said was, "Let's go, boy," before he turned and walked away.

I saw disappointment in the slump of his shoulders as he led the way out of the woods that bright fall morning. I stumbled after him, saddened by the knowledge that I had failed him once again.

Sunday was as uneventful as Saturday. I slept late again, having put a sizeable dent in Herbie's Beefeater bottle the night before when such thoughts of my childhood had kept me awake long past my normal bedtime. Then I spent several hours in the library with my Victorian murder before walking a few miles out of town and back. Walking, I have found, helps me to clarify my thoughts. At least it usually does, though on this occasion they were not noticeably clearer when I got back to my apartment.

9

Ben Latta was waiting for me when I got out of my nine o'clock class Monday morning. The day had gone more or less normally, except that almost everyone had heard about my father's death and wanted to offer condolences. It got to be tiring after a while, and my response soon became mechanical.

"I was sorry to hear about your father," Ben said after he was seated in the stuffed chair.

"Thanks, Ben. We've all got to go some time, and his time had come." It sounded callous, even to my ears, and Ben gave me a sharp look.

"What's been happening with the James-Tyrell case?" I asked, before he could start in on me.

"Not a whole hell of a lot, actually."

"Come on, Ben. Something must have happened, or you wouldn't have let Harrison loose."

He waved that away with a flip of his hand. "That's old hat. We're concentrating on the victim's background now, trying to find a motive for the killing—"

"Wait a minute, now. It may be old hat to you, but the last time we talked—except for our run-in Wednesday night," I amended with a grin, trying to make light of it, "—you had Harrison in your clutches and were showing no signs of letting him go. What happened?"

He surprised me by exploding. "Damn it all, John, will you let me ask the questions?" He must have been under considerable pressure, because he was normally one of the most even-tempered people I had ever known. I was startled at the outburst, and a little offended as well, until I caught a glimpse of what it must have looked like from his side. He was my friend, sure, but he was also a cop, and at the moment being a cop took precedence. I didn't absorb all this at once, however, and the conversation was unnaturally formal for a few minutes.

"Tell me again about the run-in between Dr. James-Tyrell and Dr. Roeder," he ground out between clenched teeth.

"What's to tell?" I began, but when I saw his jaw muscles tighten I decided to humor him. I went through the details of the chairmanship dust-up once more.

When I finished, he asked, "And what about lately? Are you sure you haven't heard anything about a more recent flare-up? Maybe not even related to the chairmanship episode?"

"Not a peep, Ben. Honest." I wondered what he was getting at, but I didn't dare ask.

"What about Kenneth Phillips?" he asked after a short pause, during which he had chewed at his lower lip while glaring distractedly at a large crack in the plaster on the wall to my left. "Have you heard anything, perhaps from your students, which might link him and Marian James-Tyrell?"

"Well, as I told you before, he is an English major, so I suppose he's taken a good many classes from her, but beyond that I couldn't say. But, then," I added, "my students don't usually talk to me about each other. They talk about themselves, or about their courses, but they save their gossip for each other, I suppose.

"I can tell you this, though—Phillips is a strong student with a good grade point, so I doubt that he had any grade problems with Marian, if that's what you're thinking." I knew that it wasn't the instant I said it, and I had that embarrassed feeling that I usually get when I say something stupid. Ben would have checked Phillips' academic record if he'd wanted information of that sort; he wouldn't have bothered to ask me.

He didn't set me straight, though. Instead, he said, "You know of no other contact between them except in the classroom?"

I shook my head.

He changed tacks abruptly. "Did you ever know James to run around on his wife?" he asked.

"Absolutely not."

"How come all the certainty? Are you and James so close that he tells you his most intimate secrets?"

"Of course not," I replied. "I don't mean that I'm certain that he never did, only that I've never seen or heard even the slightest suggestion that he had ever done so."

Ben shook his head resignedly, as though he had heard that answer many times before. Then he asked, "What about Sally Rhinemann?"

I laughed out loud. "So someone's been bandying that old chestnut about, have they?"

He didn't respond. He just sat there, waiting for an answer.

So I gave it to him. "Sally Rhinemann is . . . " I searched for the right word. "She's, well, spacey is about the best way to describe her, though it pains me to use that faddish word. As a librarian she's all right, I suppose. At least I've never heard any complaints about her. But when she gets out away from the stacks and the card catalogs she's not very reliable."

Ben was listening intently, though I couldn't imagine that I had any information that would be of use to him.

"As you have apparently already learned," I continued, "she is interested in the theater. Several years ago she had the romantic lead in a play opposite Harrison James, and she seemed to think that they should carry on the relationship off stage as well as on. She gave Harrison quite a time of it, so the story goes, and it was at least a semester before he could go to the library without having to keep a careful eye peeled for her.

"Now Sally, as you know if you've seen her, is a remarkably attractive woman, and there aren't many men who would dodge if she threw herself at them. But Harrison did. If you're thinking that Harrison might have wanted to get rid of Marian in order to make way for Sally, you couldn't be more mistaken."

"Yeah?" Ben said. "But what about Sally? Mightn't she have wanted to get rid of Marian in order to get James for herself?"

I had not thought of that, but it didn't seem likely. I told Ben so, adding, "Sally's a bit flakey, but she's not crazy. I'm sure that Harrison never encouraged her, and besides, that was all over ages ago."

"Apparently not," Ben said. "Sally Rhinemann has the female

lead in this year's production as well, and last Tuesday night, about an hour before Marian James-Tyrell was killed, she stormed out of rehearsal muttering threats against her."

I groaned. "For God's sake, Ben, she's just a frustrated actress who wants everything to be larger than life. She was just posturing, I'm sure. She wouldn't hurt anyone. The idea of Sally Rhinemann as a murderer is downright laughable."

Ben wasn't laughing. "If murderers all looked and acted like murderers," he said, "my job would be a hell of a lot easier. She wouldn't be the first beautiful, flighty young woman to become a killer. You yourself have doubts about her mental stability—"

"Wait, now, I didn't say that—"

"You said she was spacey," Ben interrupted, looking at his notes, "and flakey and unreliable. She could be more than that. Besides, she has no alibi. She says she drove around for several hours trying to cool down, but nobody noticed her if she did. Her mother was sound asleep when she got home, whenever that was, so she has no alibi whatever."

"You've obviously questioned her; do you really think she could be a murderer?" I asked in my most incredulous tone.

"Anybody can be a murderer, John, given the proper motivation. And she still insists that she loves James."

"Jesus Christ!" I muttered. Ben might consider Sally a suspect, but I didn't. In many ways she was just a child, exasperating at times, but with no harm in her. In her late twenties, but looking much younger, Sally was still something of a mystery to me. As I had told Ben, she was a fully trained librarian who performed her duties well enough, but there were times when dealing with her was very much like dealing with a child— especially for men.

She was a native of Brookleigh, had attended high school and later college here, and still lived at home with her elderly widowed mother. Despite her great beauty, she didn't have much of a social life, and her chronic innocence and naïveté seemed to be the cause. As I had suggested to Ben, most men in my acquaintance would have leaped at the opportunity of a casual romp in the hay with someone as attractive as Sally. In fact, however, her innocence was so great that her beauty seemed almost asexual. Her fine features, luxurious blonde hair, and radiant smile more befitted an angel than a seductress. My impression was that, for Sally, casual sex under any circumstances was completely unthinkable. For her, sex and love were inseparable. Which was why, I supposed, she had thrown herself at Harrison so completely. She was convinced that she loved him, therefore she wanted to give herself to him completely, even though he was a married man.

Had been a married man, I corrected myself. He was now a widower. I wondered briefly whether there might be something to Ben's suspicions after all.

Ben switched tacks on me again. "What do you know about bad blood between Marian James-Tyrell and Glen Riddle?"

"Riddle?" I asked, taken completely by surprise. Then I thought I saw the connection. To try to get back on Ben's good side, I decided to give him as complete an answer as I could manage. This was made easier for me by the fact that I didn't particularly like Glen Riddle.

"He's one of our rising administrative stars," I began. "He started out as a recruiter for the college immediately after his graduation back in the mid-sixties. Within a couple of years he had become director of recruitment. He was a real hotshot. He worked on his master's degree at night, and soon after he acquired it he was made director of development—that is, chief fund-raiser, next to the president of the college.

"He left Brookleigh for a while in the seventies—he was hired away by another college—and while he was gone he acquired a doctorate in education. Two years ago he returned to Brookleigh as President Wilkerson's administrative assistant, and rumor has it that he is being groomed as Wilkerson's replacement, when he retires a couple of years from now."

"Okay," Ben said, impatiently. "That's who he is. Now tell me what you know about him and Marian James-Tyrell."

"I was getting to that, Ben. I thought you wanted me to be thorough."

He managed a slight smile and said, "Get on with it."

"All right. Last year Riddle represented Wilkerson at several faculty meetings and took some pretty heavy abuse from Marian over the administration's unwillingness to fund a remedial reading program. So far as I know, there was no further open conflict between them, but on that one occasion Marian tongue-lashed him to within an inch of his life. They both pointedly avoided each other's company from then on."

I almost stopped there, but I decided to give Ben every scrap that I had. "There's one other thing that might interest you, Ben. Recently someone started a rumor that Riddle, who is a married man with three young children, has been running around on his wife, but I don't believe for a moment that Marian was the source. She just wasn't the kind of person to spread malicious rumors. Besides, I hardly think that Riddle would kill someone just for spreading a rumor."

"There you go again," Ben said. "From what you've said, Riddle is a highly ambitious man. Couldn't a rumor like that—especially if there was any truth to it—seriously hinder his efforts to advance in the college administration?"

I admitted that it could.

"Well, there you are. The graveyards are full of people who were killed for motives much weaker than that. And, wouldn't you know it, Riddle doesn't have an alibi for the night of the murder, either. Says he was working late on some reports and didn't get home until about twelve-thirty. His wife confirms that he was there by then, but he could have killed Marian James-Tyrell and gotten home in time without too much difficulty. So Riddle's still in it, too.

"Well," he said, rising from the chair, "I've got some more questions to ask of some other people, so I'll be getting along."

The tension between us had dispelled as we talked, and we seemed to be back to normal. Still, I didn't want to risk another outburst, so I refrained, though not without difficulty, from renewing my question about the evidence that had led to Harrison's release.

"Things have pretty much ground to a halt with this investigation," Ben said as he prepared to leave, "so if nothing happens in the meantime I'll probably be able to make it to class Wednesday night. Did I miss much last week?"

"A few hundred years," I said. "We covered the Hundred Years' War and the Wars of the Roses. But the real excitement should be this Wednesday night." I explained that we were going to spend some time discussing the question of Richard III and the princes in the Tower. "It ought to be right down your alley," I said, "with murders, missing bodies, and the like."

"Yeah," he said. "As if I didn't get my fill of crime during the daytime." When he left we were both smiling, our friendship back on its usual even keel.

After Ben's departure I thought some more about Marian's murder. Except for whatever it was that led the police to release Harrison, there were apparently no substantial clues beyond what had been discovered at the murder scene early Wednesday morning, and that evidence, it seemed to me, could be interpreted in only one of two ways. Either there was an intruder, whom Harrison had surprised in the act of killing Marian, or there was no intruder and Harrison was himself the murderer. The police seemed to have rejected the latter possibility, at least for the time being, though for what reason I could not imagine.

If Harrison was not the murderer, it would appear that the intruder had entered the Tyrell mansion for the express purpose of killing Marian. There was no suggestion that her death had been an unfortunate consequence of a burglary. Nothing had been reported taken from the Tyrell mansion. And, far from surprising a burglar at his occupation, Marian herself had clearly been surprised while lying in bed. Whoever had killed her had done so deliberately, not in a moment of panic.

So the murderer must have been someone who had a reason for wanting her dead. From Ben's questions I thought I could identify the principal suspects: Katie Roeder, whose motive could have been jealousy and revenge; Glen Riddle, who might have killed her to protect his career; Sally Rhinemann, who might have murdered to get her hands on Harrison; and Kenneth Phillips, who . . . . I had no idea what motive Phillips might have had, and I made a mental note to ask around about him the first opportunity I got.

Then, of course, there was Harrison himself. I didn't have to try to think of a motive for him; nowadays it seems that the mere fact of being married constitutes sufficient motive for murder. Whenever someone is murdered, the spouse immediately becomes the prime suspect until, as in Harrison's case, evidence is unearthed to establish the spouse's innocence.

Damn it all, I thought, what *was* it that caused the police to let Harrison go?

10

I spent the rest of that Monday plying my trade. I had given an exam to my nine o'clock class, and I graded the papers during my spare time throughout the day. Interruptions for classes, lunch, and coffee kept me from progressing very rapidly, so when the day ended I took the ungraded balance home with me. As an undergraduate, one of my biggest peeves had been the professor who gave an exam and then waited weeks before getting it back to his students, leaving them on tenterhooks wondering how they had done. I kept that in mind when I moved to the other side of the lectern, and I always tried to give exams back to my students at the class meeting following the test.

There was another reason for tackling the exams right away. I had always felt that the best way to deal with unpleasant tasks was to do them immediately—they never went away on their own, and it only prolonged the discomfort to postpone them— and grading exams and papers was the most unpleasant part of my job. This was partly because I didn't enjoy sitting in judgment of others. The process of assigning grades was so subjective as sometimes to seem arbitrary. Not that it was difficult to separate the passing efforts from the failing, but the dividing line between a high B and a low A was anything but well drawn, and I was not so assured of my own infallibility that I could assign A's and B's and C's with complete equanimity.

Another part of the reason was the appallingly poor performance of the students. When I had begun teaching, there was a noticeable difference in the quality of work my students produced and what had been normal when I began my undergraduate studies. Since then the decline had continued and had even increased. So, grading examinations and papers in which complete sentences were rare and misspellings and grammatical errors were abundant was a gut-wrenching experience.

It wasn't just the quality of the writing that was disturbing; the quality of the thinking had also plummeted, and I had gained a reputation for being one of the toughest teachers on campus because I continued to grade by what I considered college-level standards. My classes were considerably smaller than those of my colleagues, especially when more than one of us offered the same course, and my pass/fail ratio had been the subject of more than one discussion with the academic dean. I had stuck to my principles, though, and continued to apply high standards. But I wasn't kidding myself; the handwriting was on the wall, and someday, possibly someday quite soon, I was going to have to go with the current and relax my standards or I was going to find myself in the midst of my less fortunate brothers, outside looking in.

I really didn't know what I would do when the crunch came. I believed very deeply in the value of education, and I knew that relaxing standards would inevitably render education worthless. I didn't want to become a party to the prostitution of a profession I loved; on the other hand, I had no delusions about what opportunities there were for former liberal arts professors in the cold, cruel world outside of academe—there weren't any. Period.

The choice, when it came, would be between Quixote or Quisling, and I was damned whichever I chose. I would put it off as long as possible, though, and do whatever I could to convince my students that an earned C was of far more value than an unearned A. There were, I knew, a few students out there who agreed with me. On occasion, students, mostly adults, had come up to me at the end of a semester to say that they had learned more getting a B or a C in one of my course than in several A courses combined. That could be taken several ways, perhaps, but I preferred to think that they meant it positively. After all, the purpose of education is to increase knowledge and thinking ability, and, as with most things in life, you get out of education in proportion to what you put into it. If I caused a student to put more work into earning an A in one of my courses than he would have had to in someone else's course, then I had caused him to learn more, to get more out of his education. It seemed to me a fair trade.

Exhausted, I finally finished the last exam about midnight, and I was sound asleep moments after my head hit the pillow. If I had any dreams, I don't remember them. It's just as well; after what I had been reading all day they would probably have been filled with Irish revolutionaries dressed in Japanese uniforms jabbering in ungrammatical English about the need to overthrow the Russian Imperial government.

I had no classes Tuesday, so I spent the morning in the library with my Victorian murder. I had trouble concentrating on it, however, since our more recent murder kept bullying its way into my mind. Fascinating though the Victorian case was, it was already a hundred and fifty years old and the trail wasn't likely to get appreciably colder if I neglected it for a while longer. So, after catching myself for the third time in as many minutes staring unseeingly at an illustrated advertisement for ladies' boots, I switched off the microfilm viewer and rewound the film. I had no illusions about being a detective, but there were some aspects of the James-Tyrell case which intrigued me, and I couldn't see any harm in trying to satisfy my curiosity. I had always had a habit of wanting explanations for things I didn't understand.

Being in the library, I decided to stop by and have a word with Sally Rhinemann. Our relationship had always been friendly, if somewhat distant. I was amused and annoyed in more or less equal parts by her non sequiturs, and I was often uncomfortable with the fact that her beautiful face and body housed such a child-like personality—it made me feel like a particularly dirty old man whenever thoughts of the impure variety stole into my mind, as they frequently did when she was around. For her part, she treated me with the same cheerful friendliness she extended to everyone she had dealings with.

That Tuesday morning, though, she was uncharacteristically

subdued. She gave me a smile when I asked if I could have a word with her, but its wattage was unusually low. As we walked back to her glass-fronted office, I realized that I hadn't the faintest idea how to start. I couldn't just blurt out a question like "Did you kill Marian James-Tyrell because you wanted her husband?" I couldn't even ask her if there was anything between her and Harrison James. I realized that I had no right to be asking her any questions at all. It dawned on me, a bit late under the circumstances, that murder investigation was not a game and ought to be left to the professionals. By the time we reached her office I was searching my brain for some innocuous question to account for my having approached her when she saved me the trouble.

"Oh, Dr. Forest," she said to me in obvious distress, "what am I to do?"

Not knowing exactly what she was referring to, I did my best to look wise and avuncular while maintaining a studied silence.

"I'm afraid," she went on after a moment, "that I've made an awful fool of myself."

That was, I thought, a hopeful sign; a little coming to grips with the world about her would do Sally a considerable amount of good.

"Tell me about it," I said, trying my damnedest to sound like Robert Young.

"Well," she said, "I've been infatuated with Harrison—Dr. James—for years. He's such a handsome man and a marvelously good actor that I fell in love with him a couple of years ago when we were in *Romeo and Juliet* together. After a while I realized that he didn't love me and I tried to forget him, but then this latest play came along, and I was with him almost every night, and all those feelings came flooding back. I told him last week that I loved him, and he lashed out at me at rehearsal."

She paused briefly for a breath before plunging on.

"He cursed me, Dr. Forest! He actually *cursed* me! He said, 'Damn it, Sally, leave me alone. I'm a married man.' Well, of course I was hurt, but I couldn't blame him. It was *her* that I blamed. His awful wife. She was the reason he didn't love me, I thought. And I'm afraid I made some threats against her when I ran from the theater in tears. But I didn't mean them, Dr. Forest. Honestly I didn't. I was thoroughly ashamed of myself by the time I got home, and I didn't know how I could ever face the other members of the cast again. And then the next day I learned that she was dead. And for a moment I was glad—oh, I'm so ashamed." She broke down here and sobbed a bit.

For a moment, when she was speaking of Marian, her tone was venomous, hinting at a mean streak I had not before suspected. But the impression was fleeting.

I stopped short of going across the room and offering her a shoulder to cry on, but only just. After a few moments she rubbed her knuckles in her eyes, for all the world like a little girl, stiffened her back, sniffed loudly a couple of times, and began to compose herself. Before she could begin to wonder what I was up to, I asked her if Harrison had ever encouraged her to think that he reciprocated her feelings.

"At play practices he did. He held me in his arms, told me that his life would not be worth living without my love, and kissed me with such passion that I nearly fainted."

I had seen that play, too, and I recognized the scene. "No, no, Sally," I said impatiently. "I don't mean when he was acting. I mean did he ever, off stage, lead you to think that he loved you, or encourage you to think that he would ever marry you?"

"Why of course not, Dr. Forest." She seemed to be startled at the notion. "How could he? He was a married man."

I groaned inwardly, thinking that maybe Ben was right; no one could possibly be that naïve. The rest of the conversation was no improvement, and I finally disentangled myself and headed for the door, unsure whether I could take much more of Sally Rhinemann and her fairy-tale world. As I left the office her voice followed me.

"Wait, Dr. Forest! What did you want to talk to me about?"

I pretended not to hear her and got out of the library before she could catch up with me. I was no longer sure that Sally could not be a murderer, but I had come away with one conviction—that she had it entirely within her power to make herself a victim.

Walking back to my office, I couldn't see that I had accomplished very much with my talk with Sally, but it had whetted my appetite for more information about the case. Nothing on earth could have lured me back to another face-to-face encounter with her, so that left three other outstanding suspects: Katie Roeder, Glen Riddle, and Kenneth Phillips.

Phillips intrigued me. I knew nothing about him besides the fact that he was a nice-looking, well-built young English major who had taken several courses from me. Getting information on him might be difficult, I thought. I didn't know who his friends were, and even if I could find out I doubted that they would tell me anything of use. There was still some distance between students and faculty members — as indeed there had to be if a decent learning environment was to be maintained — and I couldn't picture any students I didn't know well coming across with any useful information. Still, I thought, there were a few with whom I was on fairly friendly terms, and one of them might be able to tell me something.

Back in my office, I was about to call one at his dormitory when an easier way came to mind. Ben had been asking about Phillips as early as last Wednesday morning, and it was next to impossible that Corinne had not gotten onto the Phillips angle and come up with something.

I had, in fact, been thinking about calling her for reasons not at all connected with the case. She had telephoned me twice since the break-up, but I had not called her at all. One doesn't keep score in these matters, but it seemed unlikely that she would keep calling without some reciprocation on my part. Indeed, I had concluded that the next move was up to me and that if I never made it what little progress we had made would soon evaporate. The question was whether I wanted to keep that from happening. At the time of the split we had both been delighted to be rid of each other. Had anything changed since then? Did I want anything to change? I didn't know, but I didn't want just to let things die. A phone call on some reasonable pretext would keep it alive until I could make up my mind, and Kenneth Phillips was as good a pretext as any.

I telephoned the newspaper office, afraid she might not be in. But luck was with me.

"Corinne Blakely," she said when I got her extension. "May I help you?" Her voice was cool and professional.

"Hello, Corinne. This is John." My throat felt a little tight, so I cleared it before going on.

"Hi, John. What can I do for you?" Some of the coolness went out of her voice, but not all of it.

"Well, I know that I'm just being nosey, but Ben Latta has asked me several times if I knew of any connection between Kenneth Phillips and Marian James-Tyrell, and my curiosity is about to kill me — if you'll pardon the expression. I hate to go around snooping in the lives of my students, and it occurred to me that you had probably learned something."

"Meaning that *I* don't mind snooping in the lives of your students?" she asked.

It was the sort of thing we used to kid about, but I didn't know how she might respond under the present circumstances. I decided to take a chance.

"Something like that," I said, and was immediately relieved to hear her laughter on the other end of the line. I was astonished that I could ever have forgotten that bubbly, joyful laugh.

"As a matter of fact," she said, "I did have a word with some of his fraternity brothers, not to mention a co-ed or two. I'm surprised that you haven't heard about it on your end."

I was puzzled. "My end?" I asked.

"Sure," she replied. "The faculty end. I should think that an affair between a student and a married professor would be a hot item on the faculty grapevine."

I was startled. I knew that Marian used to have an occasional fling, but it never occurred to me that she would have become involved with a student.

"You mean Marian and this Phillips boy were having an affair?" I was incredulous. "Why, Marian was a good fifteen years older than he is."

"Sixteen, actually. But what's so terrible about that? Plenty of men get involved with girls half their age without causing too many raised eyebrows. Why should it be any different for women? You're not turning into a male chauvinist on me, are you John?"

I was so pleased with the possessive construction of that last sentence that I let the bastardization of the word chauvinist pass without my usual tirade on the necessity of treating the language with respect.

"Turning into one, hell. I never was anything else." That wasn't true — well, not entirely — but it was the snappiest repartee I could come up with at the moment. "What can you tell me?" I asked.

"Well," she began, "it appears that Kenneth Phillips was smitten by Marian James-Tyrell almost from the first day of his college career. He took both semesters of freshman English from her, and at the end of his first year he changed his major from pre-law to English. Since then, he has taken every course that Dr. James-Tyrell has taught, including some independent-study courses."

"Hmmm," I interposed. "I think I see it coming."

"You do," she agreed. "It was during one of those courses that the affair had its brief flowering. Dr. James-Tyrell had apparently treated Phillips' infatuation with amused tolerance for the first couple of years, but he is a strikingly handsome young man, and finally, one afternoon while they were alone in her office, she allowed him to kiss her. From that point she allowed other things as well, but after a week or so of clandestine meetings she decided that the affair could ultimately bring her nothing but trouble and broke it off."

"Where on earth did you get this information? Did you talk to Phillips direct?"

"I did talk to him, yes, but not about the intimate details. Those I got from his girl friend, Margaret."

"His girl friend?" I repeated, puzzled. "Oh, you mean after Marian broke it off."

"Actually," Corinne corrected me, "she's been his girl friend ever since his sophomore year. Phillips, it would seem, is not the faithful type. In fact, he appears to have kept Margaret *au courant* of his torrid romance with Dr. James-Tyrell." There was a hint of strong disapproval in Corinne's voice.

"The beast!" I said teasingly.

There was a brief pause, but Corinne declined to rise to the bait. Ignoring my comment, she continued.

"Phillips apparently took his rejection very hard. For years he had yearned for Dr. James-Tyrell, and to have her briefly only to lose her was almost more than his delicate spirit could bear." Her voice dripped with sarcasm. "After a month or two, during which his school work suffered grievously, he managed to pull together the tattered remnants of his self-esteem and get on with his life. In fact, he recovered to the point of being able to take classes from her without obvious discomfort."

"Well, well, well," I said, originally, as I digested what I had just heard. "So that's why Ben is interested in Phillips. I don't suppose you know whether he has an alibi for last Tuesday night and early Wednesday morning, do you?"

"He says he was in his room at the fraternity house, fast asleep," she replied. "Unfortunately, his roommate tied one on that night and was unconscious until the next morning and can't confirm his story. Phillips could have left the house quite easily without being seen."

"Are you going to be able to use any of this in the paper?" I asked when it became evident that she had run dry.

"Damned little. My editor is the kind of fellow who sees law suits behind every tree and under every bed, and if there is the slightest chance that something in a story might cause the paper legal problems he cuts it out."

"Makes upholding the public's right to know a little difficult, eh?"

"Right," she agreed with a chuckle.

"Well," I said, "I'll let you get back to work. Thanks for all the gossip."

"Any time," she said, and she sounded as though she meant it.

Part II
Interruption

11

I arrived at my Wednesday evening class at six-thirty on the dot. As I stood behind the lectern, waiting for the various conversations in the room to be brought to a hurried, whispered conclusion, I saw that Ben's usual seat toward the rear of the class was empty. I wondered if anything had come up in the James-Tyrell case to keep him away. Kenneth Phillips was in his accustomed place, looking politely bored as he thumbed through the pages of his notebook. He was, as Corinne had observed, a handsome young man, and, given Marian's sensual nature, I supposed it wasn't all that surprising that she had momentarily yielded to his attentions.

When the last conversation came to its sibilant end, I spoke. "As I promised last week, tonight we are going to take a good, long look at the question of Richard III and the princes in the Tower. Last week Mr. Warren gave us a spirited and persuasive presentation of the basic positions taken by Richard's supporters. Since then several of you have delved more deeply into certain aspects of the question, and I'll be asking you to enlighten us about your discoveries shortly. Before I do, however, I'd like to say a few words about the traditional version of the events Mr.

Warren described last week—that is, the version professional historians have propounded down through the years.

"First, notwithstanding the efforts of Josephine Tey and her cohorts to pretend otherwise, it has been centuries since any reputable historian has attempted to portray Richard as a monster. That thesis has been kept alive mainly by Shakespeare's play and by the Richardists themselves, who find it easier to convince others that Richard was not a monster than to convince them that he was not simply a man whose ambition led him to the commission of crimes. The blacker they can pretend that traditional historians have painted Richard, the easier it is for them to show that such a picture is false.

"In fact, the traditional version does not differ much from that of the Richardists as to events, but it does differ greatly as to how those events are interpreted. The traditional version does not deny that Richard had served his brother faithfully and well throughout Edward's reign, nor does it assert that in the days immediately following the king's death Richard embarked at once on his scheme to usurp the crown for himself. Rather, it suggests that in those early days the intrigues of the Woodville faction—the Woodvilles, you will recall, being the grasping family of Edward's widow, Elizabeth—caused Richard to take drastic actions to preserve the rightful powers of lord protector which he had been granted in Edward IV's will. These actions included the seizure of the person of the young king and the arrest of his Woodvillian guardians on the thirtieth of April, which precipitated the flight of the remaining members of the faction into exile or sanctuary.

"Until this point, Richard had had the support of William, Lord Hastings, one of Edward IV's closest friends and allies and a staunch foe of the Woodville faction. Whether, as the Richardists would have it, Hastings became dissatisfied with his prospects under Richard and began to intrigue with the enemies of the lord protector, or, as the traditional version goes, Hastings made it clear that he would not be a party to any act which would deprive the son of his late king of his rightful inheritance, Richard resolved to remove Hastings before his intrigues could bear fruit. Accordingly, during an ordinary visit of Hastings and several others to the Tower, Richard pretended to discover them plotting against his life and had Hastings beheaded that same day and the others placed under arrest—"

"Dr. Forest?"

"Yes, Mr. Warren?"

"Hastings was not executed the same day of his arrest; he was given a fair trial and was not executed until a week later."

"So the Richardists say. But the evidence does not support that contention."

"But it does, sir. Tey refers to a contemporary letter which gives the date of Hastings' arrest as the twentieth of June, and he wasn't executed until a week later."

"Sorry, Mr. Warren, but Tey made an out-and-out blunder there. Her contention that Hastings was arrested on the twentieth and not executed until the twenty-seventh is completely contradicted by the very letter to which she refers. You couldn't know that, Mr. Warren, because Tey, characteristically, does not identify the letter, nor does she quote from it. She merely says that it exists and that it places Hastings' arrest on the twentieth and his execution a week later."

I addressed the class at large: "Who had the Hanham article?"

A middle-aged woman in a nurse's uniform timidly raised her hand.

I continued. "Allison Hanham addressed the question of the date of Hastings' death in an article entitled 'Richard III, Lord Hastings and the Historians' which appeared in *The English Historical Review* in 1972. In it she quotes the letter to which Tey refers. Tell us about the letter, Mrs. Crick."

"Well, sir, the letter, written in London on Saturday, June twenty-first, is from Simon Stallworthe to Sir William Stonor. If you'll give me a moment I'll find the relevant portion. Yes, here it is. Stallworthe writes, 'On Friday last was the Lord Chamberlain'—that's Lord Hastings—'headed soon upon noon. On Monday last was at Westminster great plenty of harnessed men. There was the deliverance of the duke of York to my lord cardinal, my lord chancellor and other many lords temporal.' "

"Thank you, Mrs. Crick. Now the obvious point here is that the letter, dated the twenty-first, speaks of Hastings having been 'headed'—by which is meant beheaded—on 'Friday last,' and, whatever interpretation is put on the phrase 'Friday last,' the one thing it cannot possibly mean is that Hastings was executed on the twenty-seventh—a full six days *after* the date of the letter. Tey is guilty of colossal carelessness. I don't want to dwell over-long on this mistake, but it does seem that a person as intent as Tey was on pointing out the alleged mistakes and deceptions of historians ought to have been a bit more careful herself.

"As for the letter itself, the 'Friday last' has traditionally been taken to mean not the twentieth of June—otherwise Stallworthe would in all likelihood have written 'yesterday' instead—but the previous Friday, the thirteenth of June. This interpretation is supported by the next sentence in the letter, which says that 'on Monday last' the duke of York was released from sanctuary. That event took place on Monday, June sixteenth, and it is logical to assume that Stallworthe was relating the events in the order in which they occurred.

"There is some internal evidence which suggests that the letter was in fact begun earlier in the week and only completed on Saturday the twenty-first. If that were the case, there would be no ambiguity whatever as to exactly which Friday was being referred to.

"Nevertheless, in the late nineteenth century Sir Clements Markham, the leading Richardist of all time and the man from whom Tey cribbed all of her information without giving him a word of credit, asserted that 'Friday last' means precisely that, the last Friday being the day before the letter was dated, or the twentieth of June. Markham, however, agreed with the traditional dating of Hastings' arrest on the thirteenth and used the Stonor letter to assert that Hastings was not executed until a week later, during which period Markham would have us believe—*on no evidence whatever*—Hastings was given a fair and orderly trial. Tey simply misread Markham's argument and assigned the arrest to the twentieth, rather than to the thirteenth, which even Markham admitted was the correct date."

Mrs. Crick was excitedly waving her hand, trying to get my attention.

"Yes, Mrs. Crick?"

"Dr. Forest, Hanham proves Hastings was not arrested on the thirteenth at all. She cites two entries in the day-by-day records of the London mercers' company, whatever that was. One of these indicates that the arrests and execution took place later than June fifteenth, and the other strongly suggests that they took place on Friday, June twentieth."

"Unfortunately, Mrs. Crick, that evidence is not as conclusive as we would like. Two years after Hanham's article appeared,

The English Historical Review ran an article entitled 'When and Why Did Hastings Lose His Head?' by B.P. Wolffe, in which Wolffe points out that the records Hanham was quoting from were copies, rather than the original documents, and that, since other pages in the same source have been shown to have been ascribed to the wrong years, there is every possibilities that these entries, dated June 1483, may actually pertain to an earlier year. The entries Hanham cites are vague and inconclusive. The first merely indicates that the lord chancellor, the bishop of Ely, and the lord chamberlain attended a meeting on the fifteenth of June. If this meeting occurred in 1483, then obviously Hastings, the lord chancellor, could not have been killed two days earlier. The second alludes to the instructions of the lord mayor of London on June twentieth to be especially careful in keeping the watch; Hanham concludes that it was the unrest following the execution of Hastings on that day that produced the order, but such orders were not uncommon in this period, and this particular order may easily have been issued on the twentieth of June of an earlier year.

"So, what evidence do we have about Hastings' arrest and execution? We have several contemporary sources—the chronicle and the legal documents—which set his death on the thirteenth; we have an ambiguous letter which can be read to say that he died on either the thirteenth or the twentieth, depending on your preference; and we have some entries in the mercers' company records which would indicate that Hastings was not executed until the twentieth, if it could be proved that the records belong to the year 1483, which it can't. As so often is the case in history, our evidence is scanty and inconsistent, and the best we can do is examine the evidence closely and go with what seems most likely, until some new information comes along to confirm or contradict our conclusions. At this point, the strongest evidence points toward Hastings having been arrested and executed on June thirteenth."

"Dr. Forest?"

"Yes, Mr. Watkins?" I said to an elderly black man at the back of the room.

"I'm not sure that I understand what difference it makes whether Hastings was executed on the day of his arrest or a week later. What does that have to do with who murdered the princes?"

"It doesn't have anything to do, directly, with the question of who murdered the princes, but it has a great deal to do with the state of mind Richard was in shortly before he seized the throne. If, as the Richardists contend, Hastings was arrested, given an orderly trial, and not executed until a week later, then the impression one gets of Richard is that of a calm, reasonable man, willing to let the wheels of justice turn at their own pace. If, on the other hand, Richard had Hastings arrested and then executed more or less on the spot, it shows a decidedly more ruthless Richard, a man willing to take bold and violent action against those who stood in his way. The point is, therefore, an important one."

"I see," Watkins said. "So the important question is whether his arrest and execution occurred on the same day or a week apart, and it really doesn't matter whether he died on the thirteenth or the twentieth."

"Actually, it does matter—" I began, but Warren interrupted me.

"You bet it matters," he said. "There is no dispute whatever regarding the date the young duke of York was released from sanctuary. It was on the sixteenth of June. If, as Dr. Forest and his fellow professional historians allege, Hastings was arrested and executed on the thirteenth of June, then they are asking us to believe that Queen Elizabeth would willingly have turned her young son over to the man who had ruthlessly executed a former friend only three days earlier. Now, can anyone possibly believe that a mother would do that?"

"That's an interesting point, Mr. Warren. In fact, it is one of the most telling arguments the Richardists have been able to muster. Certainly the traditional version would be more convincing with Hastings being arrested and executed on the twentieth, four days after the release of the duke of York, rather than the thirteenth, three days before. The Richardists, on the other hand, would be happiest with Hastings being arrested on the thirteenth but not executed until the twentieth. What evidence there is, however, supports neither of these scenarios: in all likelihood, Hastings was arrested *and* executed on June thirteenth, and we are just going to have to live with that unless and until new evidence comes to light.

"But, despite the feigned skepticism of the Richardists, Elizabeth's surrendering of the young duke of York on the sixteenth, even if it did follow by only a few days the abrupt killing of Hastings, is not inexplicable. First of all, Elizabeth's career does not suggest to us a woman whose principal concern was the well-being of her children. On the contrary, her principal concern from the beginning was the enrichment of herself in power and material goods, and this is the image of Elizabeth which the Richardists themselves promote in all but this one instance. When she is in opposition to Richard, the Richardists paint her black as night; but when, as in this case, they can make Richard look good by portraying her sympathetically, they don't hesitate to reverse themselves completely. Thus we are told that Elizabeth was a devoted mother who would never have turned her younger son over to Richard unless she knew for a certainty that the son would be perfectly safe in Richard's hands.

"The fact is, it was entirely possible that her son would have been taken from sanctuary by force had she not surrendered him willingly. The duke of Buckingham, who was allied with Richard at this point, argued persuasively that, since sanctuary was intended only for the guilty and since the young boy was clearly innocent, he could not claim sanctuary. Had Buckingham's argument held sway, and had his men, or those of Richard, violated sanctuary to the extent of taking the boy, they might easily, while there, have taken the royal treasures which Elizabeth had dragged into sanctuary with her, even if they didn't take Elizabeth herself. But by giving up the boy, whom she would have lost anyway had Buckingham had his way, she managed to keep her loot and improve her position with Richard slightly by seeming to cooperate with him.

"Another thing to consider is that Hastings had long been one of the staunchest enemies of the Woodville party, and it is entirely possible that Elizabeth viewed his execution not with alarm but with satisfaction.

"But we seem to have wandered pretty far down one of the countless paths which are strewn about all historical questions to deflect the unwary from the main course.

"To get back to the point, the elimination of Hastings seems to have been the turning point for Richard. Having with that act set out on the path of violence, his next steps came easier. With the young duke of York now safely in his hands, Richard put the next part of his plan into operation. On Sunday, June twenty-second, he had sermons preached in London on the subject of the bastardy of the two princes, so as to give Bishop Stillington's alleged 'evidence,' which Mr. Warren made much of last week, the widest possible currency. The way was thus prepared for Parliament to declare Richard of Gloucester the legitimate heir to Edward IV and to petition him to accept the crown, which was done on the twenty-fifth, and on the following day Richard fulfilled his greatest ambition by accepting the offer and becoming King Richard III.

"The only blemish on his success was the continued existence of the two princes. Perhaps Richard feared an uprising in young Edward's favor; perhaps he merely felt that the elimination of the princes was a precaution which a prudent man in his position could not fail to take. Whatever his reason, he quickly resolved on the boys' murder and had it carried out, probably within a few weeks of his acceptance of the crown.

"And that, in essence, is the traditional version, as put forth by historians in general for some time now. Notice that it does not portray Richard as a monster—merely as a man whose ambition led him to commit a crime."

"Now wait a minute," Warren interjected. "What Richard did was *not* a crime."

"To what do you refer, Mr. Warren? To his replacing Edward V on the throne of England, or to his having the princes killed?"

"He *didn't* have them killed," Warren said doggedly. "Henry VII did. But what I am referring to is his taking over as king. Since the princes were bastards, Richard III was the rightful heir to the throne, and taking what was rightfully his cannot be considered a crime."

"Ah, but *were* the princes bastards, Mr. Warren?"

"Of course. There's Stillington's evidence to prove it."

"And what, precisely, was Stillington's evidence?"

"Proof that Edward IV was already married to Eleanor Butler when he married Elizabeth Woodville. That made his marriage to Elizabeth invalid, and all offspring from an invalid marriage are illegitimate."

"But what evidence, Mr. Warren, did Stillington produce in support of his claim?"

Warren looked uncomfortable. "I'm sorry, sir. I don't know."

"Dr. Forest?" said one of my sharper young students.

"Yes, Mr. Torrelli?"

"You assigned me Mortimer Levine's 1959 *Speculum* article, 'Richard III—Usurper or Lawful King?' Levine points out that, according to the chronicle in which Stillington's so-called evidence

102

is mentioned, it was *Richard*, not Stillington, who brought forth the evidence, in the form of 'depositions of divers witnesses testifying King Edward's children to be bastards,' and that, furthermore, the source of this information, the duke of Buckingham, had this to say about the evidence: 'Which depositions then I thought to be true as now I know them to be feigned and testified by persons with rewards untruly suborned.' The Richardists, Levine goes on to point out, distort this evidence in two ways: first, by pretending that it was Stillington who produced it when in fact it was Richard; and second, by failing to point out that the man from whom we learn of the existence of this evidence had himself declared that evidence to be false."

"Thank you, Mr. Torrelli—"

"Excuse me, sir, but there's more."

"Continue, then."

"Well, sir, after Levine asks, rhetorically, 'If Richard and his cohorts were unable to produce proof of the precontract, why should it not be dismissed as a mere invention?', he goes on to point out that even if there had been a precontract—that is, even if Edward had married Eleanor Butler—Eleanor had died in 1468, while the two princes were not born until 1470 and 1473, so, while there might be some technical basis for contending that Edward's marriage to Elizabeth Woodville was irregular, it was a mere legal quibble to contend that the boys were bastards, when Eleanor Butler had been dead for two years before the first of them was born. In other words, Levine asserts that the evidence was in the first place false, and that even if it had not been false it still would not have made the princes bastards."

"That last argument," Warren interjected, "seems particularly limp to me. And as for proof, there is the direct testimony of Stillington himself. He not only says that the precontract existed, but he declares that he, Stillington, performed the marriage ceremony himself."

"It is at least possible, Mr. Warren," I said, "that Stillington lied. He had been imprisoned for a time by Edward, and he was anything but fond of the Woodvilles; he could have lied about the precontract out of a simple desire to discomfit his enemies. He wouldn't have been the first person, and certainly not the last, to give false testimony to promote the interests of a political ally. Bear in mind that it would have been a very low-risk lie: with both Eleanor Butler and Edward dead, there was little chance of anyone proving that he did not at some time or another marry them."

Ben Latta had come in as I was speaking, so I decided to give the class a short break while I asked him if there had been any new development in Marian's case.

Most of the students went out into the hall for a stretch, a smoke, or a drink of water, but Ben stayed where he was. I walked over and perched a hip on a nearby desk. When I asked my question he replied, "Not a thing. I was late getting here because a car ahead of me on Walnut ran through the Fifth Street red light and smashed into the side of a soft-drink truck. I hung around until the uniformed boys arrived, then I had to go home and change shoes after wading through all that soda pop."

We chatted idly as the room slowly filled up again, then I returned to the front.

12

When everyone had settled down again, Mrs. Payne, a middle-aged woman who seemed perpetually astonished that England had not been all bobbies and Piccadilly Circus and steak-and-kidney pie from the very beginning, imperiously waved her hand at me.

"Yes, Mrs. Payne?"

"What I don't understand is why doesn't someone look in the official records, or the newspapers, or *something*, to clear up all this confusion? Surely there's no reason for all this guessing about what happened."

"But there is plenty of reason, Mrs. Payne. These fragmentary and quite unsatisfactory sources about which we have been talking are all that remain. The fifteenth century was not a very literate age. Public records were not well kept, and many that were have been lost in the intervening centuries. As for newspapers, there weren't any. In fact, the newspaper didn't even exist in England until the late eighteenth century. So the historian is dependent upon such unsatisfactory sources as fragmentary official records, personal correspondence, and individual memoirs, where they exist."

Mrs. Payne was indignant. "Do you mean to say," she

demanded, "that there are no first-hand accounts of what went on in London during this period?"

"That is very nearly the truth, Mrs. Payne. In fact, it *was* the truth until the nineteen-thirties, when a first-hand account, written by Dominic Mancini, was discovered in the Bibliotheque Municipale at Lille, France. Mancini was an Italian clergyman who was in London from the summer of 1482 until the late summer of 1483, probably on business for the pope. He was intimate with high-ranking individuals in London and was in a position to know what was going on in England during his sojourn there. After leaving England he wrote an account of his stay, which for some reason was never published in his time, and its very existence was forgotten until a copy of the manuscript was discovered in Lille centuries later. An English translation was prepared by C.A.J. Armstrong and was published under the title *The Usurpation of Richard III* in 1936, fifteen years before Tey wrote *The Daughter of Time*. Significantly, Tey ignores it completely, though she could hardly have been ignorant of its existence."

"Well, then," Mrs. Payne asked impatiently, "what does it have to say about these events? Does it support the Richardist position or the traditional position?"

"Who had Armstrong?" I asked of the class at large. An elderly Oriental gentleman in the front row raised his hand.

"Yes, Mr. Soo, would you care to answer Mrs. Payne's question?"

"It would give me great pleasure, Dr. Forest," he said in a gentle voice in which only the trace of an accent remained. "The account of Father Mancini is essentially the same as that which has been labeled the traditional version in this discussion. The only significant point of difference is that Father Mancini places the arrest and execution of Hastings *after* the release of young Richard of York from sanctuary."

"Ha!" Warren fairly shouted. "So the only eyewitness account disagrees with the traditional version in this very important respect."

"I wouldn't be too elated, Mr. Warren. Whatever the chronology, Mancini definitely places the arrest and the execution on the same date. In fact, if I remember correctly, he makes some comment about Richard's guilt in the incident."

"That is correct, Dr. Forest," Mr. Soo said softly. "I can read the exact words, if you wish."

"Please do, sir."

"Mancini wrote, 'After this execution had been done in the citadel, the townsmen, who had heard the uproar but were uncertain of the cause, became panic-stricken, and each one seized his weapons. But, to calm the multitude, the duke' — that is, Richard, duke of Gloucester — 'sent a herald to proclaim that a plot had been detected in the citadel, and Hastings, the originator of the plot, had paid the penalty; wherefore he bade them all be reassured. At first the ignorant crowd believed, although the real truth was on the lips of many, namely that the plot had been feigned by the duke so as to escape the odium of such a crime.' "

Watkins had his hand up again, so I nodded at him.

"How is it possible, Dr. Forest, for the Richardists to argue that Hastings was executed a week after his arrest in light of this evidence?"

"Well, Mr. Watkins, the preeminent Richardist of all times was Sir Clements Markham, who did his Richardist writings in the late nineteenth and early twentieth centuries, before Mancini's account was brought to light. Later Richardists have mostly chosen to follow his lead. In fact, Tey's book is nothing but an uncredited paraphrase of Markham's work. Since Mancini largely reduces the Richardist edifice to rubble, they are confronted with a choice between abandoning much of their position or pretending that Mancini doesn't exist. They generally choose the latter; Tey certainly did."

Robert Richter raised his hand. In his thirties, he was a clerk in a convenience store I sometimes visited when I needed something at odd hours.

"Yes, Mr. Richter?"

"You said that the traditional version held that Richard had the princes done away with shortly after he took the throne. Mr. Warren says that they weren't done away with until years later, when Henry VII was king, and that there were no rumors afloat that Richard had murdered his nephews. Now, if Mancini was in England until the end of the summer, he would have been in a position to hear the rumors if in fact there *were* any rumors. My question is, did he hear any rumors, and, if so, what were they?"

"Mr. Soo?"

"Yes, Dr. Forest." Turning around so that he could see Richter, Mr. Soo said, "Father Mancini does indeed speak of rumors. If it is permitted," he glanced back at me, "I can read what he says."

"Certainly, Mr. Soo," I said. "Go right ahead."

"Father Mancini begins by remarking, 'But after Hastings was removed, all the attendants who had waited upon the king were debarred access to him. He and his brother were withdrawn into the inner apartments of the Tower proper, and day by day began to be seen more rarely behind the bars and windows, till at length they ceased to appear altogether.' Then he writes, 'I have seen many men burst forth into tears and lamentations when mention was made of him'—meaning young Edward V—'after his removal from men's sight; and already there was a suspicion that he had been done away with. Whether, however, he has been done away with, and by what manner of death, so far I have not at all discovered.' "

"That proves nothing," Warren remarked when Mr. Soo had finished reading. "That's just the word of a single man, and even he admits that he doesn't know whether the rumors are true, or even how the princes were purported to have been killed."

"But he was there, Mr. Warren," I replied. "He was in London at the time of these goings-on, and he reported on them, in these words, only a few months after they transpired. Furthermore, the people with whom he associated were not the common folk, the ordinary people of London, but the upper and upper-middle classes—in other words, the people who were most likely to know what was happening.

"Mancini is, in fact, a highly reliable witness, and if he reports that there were fears in London in the late summer of 1483 that the princes had been murdered, then we can confidently conclude that such fears were actually afoot. That doesn't mean that the princes were in fact dead, but it certainly means that the people feared that they might be. And that, coupled with the rumor recorded in the Croyland Chronicle and the rumor that reached the Continent by the first of the year, as witnessed by the speech of the French chancellor, pretty effectively dispenses with the Richardist contention that there were no rumors of murder during the reign of Richard III. There is, in fact, another reference to such rumors in the Great Chronicle of London, which, if I remember correctly, reads something like this: 'But after Easter'—that would be Easter of 1484—'much whispering was among the people that the king had put the children of King Edward to death.' As for the Richardist position that there could have been no rumors since Richard made no effort to squelch them, it conveniently overlooks the very obvious fact that if he had in fact already had the princes murdered, he was in no position to produce their live and breathing bodies to the public, which would have been the most obvious way of dispelling any such rumors. He *didn't* produce them, and certainly one plausible explanation for why he didn't was that he couldn't because they were already dead."

"But—" Warren began again.

I interrupted him. "No buts this time, Mr. Warren. The Richardists are quite happy insisting that we believe in something like Edward's precontract with Eleanor Butler, when the only evidence they can produce of its existence is declared to be false by the very person who supplies it, but they reject out of hand contemporary and eyewitness accounts which do not support their view. They apply two very different standards when evaluating the admissibility of evidence: that which supports their position is accepted as revealed truth without the slightest examination, while that which runs counter to their position is rejected as false, or biased, or inaccurate, regardless of how well it stands up under objective examination. That's the problem with the Richardists—they do the very things they accuse professional historians of doing, only they do them even more enthusiastically and unabashedly that even Sir Thomas More or William Shakespeare ever dared to do."

"Come now, Dr. Forest," Warren broke in, seeing an opening. "It is well established that Sir Thomas More didn't write that scurrilous piece of claptrap. John Morton wrote it. The only reason that anyone ever thought that More wrote it was that a manuscript copy, in More's handwriting, was found among his papers after his death. More had simply made himself a copy of the original, which was clearly written by Morton as part of his long-running attempt to vilify Richard."

"This, Mr. Warren, is a prime example of what I was just referring to. The Richardists have never—*never*—offered any proof whatever that the manuscript was not the original creation of Sir Thomas More, and their suggestion that the copy in his handwriting was one that he had penned from some mythical manuscript written by John Morton so that he'd have a copy of his own is downright laughable. In 1513, the year in which all sides agree the work was composed, the thirty-five-year-old More was a busy public official—an under-sheriff of the city of London. Had he wanted a copy of someone else's manuscript, it is flatly inconceivable that he would have taken the time to sit down and copy it out in his own hand. The work is a good thirty thousand words long, and had More wanted a copy he would certainly have had one of his subordinates do it rather than waste days of his own valuable time. The fact that the manuscript is in More's own hand is the best possible proof that he was himself the author. What's more, the *History of King Richard III* has often been called the first great prose work in the English language. It is just the sort of thing we would expect from More."

"Dr. Forest?"

"Yes, Mrs. Crick?"

"You just said that More's *History* was written in 1513."

"That date is now widely accepted, yes."

"And that More was thirty-five years old at the time."

"Yes."

"Then More must have been about five years old at the time that these events took place, so he can hardly be considered a reliable witness to them."

"That is quite correct. As a child he could only have been vaguely aware of the events at the time they were taking place. But later in his youth he served as a page in John Morton's household, and it is not unreasonable to believe that Morton spoke of the events in his presence, though he may never have sat young Thomas down and given him a blow-by-blow account of the happenings. Furthermore, though More was a small child at the time, many of his later associates were adults during Richard's reign, and it cannot be doubted that More picked the brains of individuals who were themselves contemporaries of, if not actual eyewitnesses to, the events that he describes."

Mrs. Crick continued. "Would you say, then, Dr. Forest, that More's *History* presents a reliable account of Richard's usurpation of the throne?"

I thought for a moment. "If by that you mean do I believe that it presents a reliable account of the specifics of Richard's usurpation, my answer must of course be no. Richard was not a hunchback. He didn't have a withered arm. And on, and on, and on. More made many mistakes that we can point to even today, and his account has an extreme bias against Richard.

"On the other hand, if you are asking whether I think that More was trying to give a false picture of what transpired, I would have to answer no, that Sir Thomas was not trying to deceive. It is extremely important to remember that standards of historical objectivity simply did not exist at that time, and people tended to view events about them as part of a larger scheme. More certainly colored his account of Richard III and painted him blacker than he deserved. But he did it for a purpose. It was important to Sir Thomas More and to his contemporaries to believe that good triumphed over evil and usurping tyrants were punished for their misdeeds. More and his contemporaries regarded this as a greater truth than could be achieved through mere historical objectivity, and they saw nothing whatever wrong with exaggerating the good or evil of their characters, if by so doing they could better illustrate what seemed to them to be the more important truth.

"So, while the *History* is full of distortions and inaccuracies, and while many of them were deliberate on More's part, they were not put there to deceive his readers, but rather to enlighten them.

"Naturally, with our different way of regarding truth nowadays, we have to read More's account with a certain amount of skepticism. But we would be as wrong to reject it all out of hand as we would be to accept it all as the complete, objective truth. In its particulars, More's account is suspect, but in its generalities it is very likely to be correct."

A young woman seated near the windows raised her hand.

"Yes, Miss Stanley?"

"If, as you say, More's account may be in error in particulars, and if, as Mr. Warren says, Shakespeare's play is largely based on More's account, how much credit should we give to Shakespeare's version of how the princes came to be murdered? I worked as a stagehand on last year's production of Shakespeare's *Tragedy of Richard III*, and I remember that those events are described in considerable detail."

"Yes, they are indeed. Actually, Shakespeare follows More's account quite closely, except that Shakespeare naturally presents those events as facts while More carefully states that he is merely re-telling the story as he has been able to discover it from reliable sources."

Ben Latta spoke up for the first time that evening. "What, precisely, is the More-Shakespeare version, Dr. Forest?"

"I believe Mr. Phillips had Sir Thomas. Tell us about it, Mr. Phillips."

Kenneth Phillips, who had never had much to say in my classes, looked uncomfortable at being called on. He cleared his throat loudly before he spoke.

"Well, sir, the first thing I would point out is Sir Thomas's own initial disclaimer, with which he prefaces his account of the murders. He says, 'I shall rehearse you the dolorous end of those babes, not after every way that I have heard, but after the way that I have so heard by such men and by such means as methinks it were hard but it should be true.' He then goes on to say that shortly after Richard's coronation on the sixth of July, Richard departed London for Gloucester. On the way 'his mind misgave him that, his nephews living, men would not reckon that he could have a right to the realm, he thought therefore without delay to be rid of them.' More says that Richard then wrote a letter to Sir Robert Brackenbury, Constable of the Tower, instructing him to kill the princes. Brackenbury returned a reply to the effect that he would himself die before he killed the children.

"Richard was at Warwick when he received Brackenbury's reply, and, according to Sir Thomas More, he enquired of an unnamed page whom he could trust to do the deed. The page replied that such a man lay virtually outside Richard's door at that moment—a Sir James Tyrell, an ambitious man whose rise in the ranks of officialdom had been hindered by men already close to Richard who did not wish to share the king's favor with another.

"When Richard explained his wishes, Tyrell proved perfectly willing, so Richard sent him off the following day with a letter instructing Brackenbury 'to deliver Sir James all the keys of the Tower for one night.' For the actual act itself, I'll quote Sir Thomas at length:

> For Sir James Tyrell devised that they should be murdered in their beds. To the execution whereof he appointed Miles Forest, one of the four that kept them, a fellow fleshed in murder before time. To him he joined one John Dighton, his own horsekeeper, a big, broad strong knave. Then all the others being removed from them, this Miles Forest and John Dighton about midnight (the innocent children lying in their beds) came into the chamber, and suddenly lapped them up among the bedclothes—so bewrapped them and entangled them, keeping down by force the featherbed and pillows hard unto their mouths, that within a while,

*smothered and stifled, their breaths failing, they gave up
to God their innocent souls into the joys of heaven, leaving
to the tormentors their bodies dead in the bed.*

*After the wretches perceived them—first by the
struggling with the pains of death and after, long lying
still—to be thoroughly dead, they laid their bodies naked
out upon the bed and fetched Sir James to see them. Who,
upon the sight of them, caused those murderers to bury
them at the stair-foot, meetly deep in the ground under a
great heap of stones.*

"When Tyrell reported back to Richard, the king was greatly
pleased that the deed was done, but he was bothered somewhat
that the bodies were buried 'in so vile a corner.' As a result—
and I'm quoting again—'a priest of Sir Robert Brackenbury
took up the bodies again and secretly interred them in such
place as, by the occasion of his death—for he alone knew
it—could never since come to light.' "

Here Warren interrupted. "I can't help wondering, Dr. Forest,
how More came by all this horribly incriminating information. Surely there were no eyewitnesses to *these* events."

"Mr. Phillips?"

"Actually, Dr. Forest, that was the very next thing More has
to say: 'Very truth it is and well known that at such time as Sir
James Tyrell was in the Tower, for treason committed against
the most famous Prince, King Henry the Seventh, both Dighton
and he were examined, and confessed the murder in manner
above written, but whither the bodies were removed they could
nothing tell.' And More concludes by saying, 'And thus, as I
have learned of them that much knew and little cause had to
lie.' "

"Dr. Forest?"

"Yes, Mrs. Crick?"

"Whatever happened to the three murderers—Tyrell, Forest,
and Dighton?"

"Mr. Phillips?"

"More answers the question quite succinctly: 'Miles Forest at
St. Martin's piecemeal rotted away. Dighton indeed yet walks
alive, in good possibility to be hanged ere he die. But Sir James
Tyrell died at Tower Hill, beheaded for treason.' "

"Yes," I remarked, "More is indeed succinct, but he is not
very revealing. Tyrell was executed, certainly, but only in
1502, and then for treason against Henry VII and not for his

alleged role in the deaths of the princes. And little can be made of the fates More assigns to Tyrell's two accomplices, Forest and Dighton. So even Sir Thomas's account does not show that the murderers were ever punished for their crime."

At this point Ben, who had started fidgeting soon after Phillips began to speak, all but leaped from his chair and strode quickly from the room, giving me an odd look as he passed my desk but offering no word of explanation. I thought that he must have recalled some important item of police business which needed attending to immediately, and I put the incident out of my mind the minute the door closed behind him.

My attention was brought back to the business at hand by Ricky Torrelli. "So far," he said, "we've heard lots of talk about written records and rumors and traditions and the like, but isn't there *any* concrete physical evidence at all? I read Tey's book this past weekend, and she mentions at one point that some bones had been discovered beneath a stairway during the reign of Charles II which were assumed to be those of the princes, but she doesn't say anything more about them. Was there never any effort made to determine anything about these bones?"

"Yes, Mr. Torrelli, there was, and Tey preferred to ignore it for the very simple reason that it was highly prejudicial to the story she was trying to promote. As in the case of Mancini's manuscript, the examination of the bones came long after Sir Clements Markham had departed from the controversy, so we cannot fault him for not mentioning it. But we can and must fault Tey for ignoring it, for it is inconceivable that she could have been unaware of it. Nevertheless, she follows Sir Clements slavishly—without, it bears repeating, even once acknowledging her debt to him—and since Sir Clements doesn't have much to say about the bones, neither does Tey.

"But they are very important, and they deserve our close attention. As Mr. Torrelli has pointed out, these particular bones first came to light during the reign of Charles II—in 1674, to be precise—when a staircase in or near the White Tower in the Tower of London was being torn down during some remodeling. They were assumed then to be the bones of the princes, but science had not yet progressed to the point where any significant conclusions could be drawn from their examination. After a time, King Charles ordered the bones placed in a white marble urn in Henry VII's Chapel in

Westminster Abbey. There they lay undisturbed until July 6, 1933, when the urn was at last reopened and the bones examined. A detailed report of that examination was made public in November 1933 and was published in *Archaelogica* the following year under the joint authorship of Lawrence E. Tanner and William Wright.

"Mrs. Waitt," I addressed an attractive middle-aged woman who sat immediately before my desk. "I believe you had the article. Would you please enlighten us as to its contents?"

"Yes, Dr. Forest. The examination of the remains was conducted by Professor William Wright, dean of London Hospital, and Dr. George Northcroft, past president of the British Dental Association. They observed that the bones were in a poor state of preservation, owing presumably to their being damaged during their discovery back in the seventeenth century, and that a number of non-human bones had become intermixed with them.

"Separating out the human bones, they were able to state with certainty that these bones represented the remains of two children. Judging from the size, they decided that the two children were separated in age by two or three years and that the oldest child had not yet reached the age of thirteen. The examination of the teeth and teeth sockets in the jaws gave corroboration to this, indicating that the eldest child was between twelve and thirteen years old, while the other was between nine and eleven.

"Lawrence Tanner, who wrote the historical sketch which accompanies Dr. Wright's medical report, points out that in the late summer of 1483 Edward V was just a few months short of his thirteenth birthday, while his younger brother was almost exactly ten years old.

"From all this Wright was absolutely convinced: 'The evidence that the bones in the urn are those of the princes is in my judgment as conclusive as could be desired, and definitely more conclusive than could, considering everything, have reasonably been expected. Further, their ages were such that I can say with complete confidence that their death occurred during the reign of their usurping uncle, Richard III.' "

When Mrs. Waitt concluded there was complete silence in the room, which was broken at last by a sputtering outburst from Father William Morgan, who ran the campus Newman Center. "Are we to understand, Dr. Forest, that at the time Josephine Tey published her *Daughter of Time*, Mancini's first-hand account of the events in London in the summer of 1483, as well as the report of the medical and dental examination of the bones uncovered in the time of Charles II, were known to exist and were readily available to anyone with access to a bookstore or library?"

"Any reasonable-sized library, yes."

"Then how on earth, sir, can Miss Tey have dared to ignore them when she wrote her book?"

"For one thing, Father, she couldn't very well afford to mention them, since they are so detrimental to the case she was trying to build. For another, her work, as I have said before, is nothing more than a blatant paraphrase of what Sir Clements Markham had written decades before either the bones were examined or Mancini's manuscript came to light. And for a third, the Richardists have long been adept at ignoring contrary evidence, so what Tey did had a strong precedent.

"Besides, she was actually pretty safe, since the average lay person is not going to go to the trouble of checking back against the original sources, and since professional historians have generally chosen to ignore the posturings of the Richardists rather than respond to them."

"But why haven't historians exposed the fallacies of the Richardist position in a popular forum?" the priest persisted.

"For one thing, historians are by and large a pretty reclusive bunch. They are vociferous enough among themselves and in their learned journals—which lay people never read—but they don't relate all that well to people out in the real world. And for another, who would listen to them?"

"I beg your pardon?" he said, puzzled.

"Look," I said. "If some enthusiastic dilettante came up with a plausible, but patently false, 'proof' that the sun revolves around the earth, he would get a great deal of attention. For one thing, it would be something unusual, something different; for another, he would be sticking his thumb in the eye of the scientific establishment, which is something that most lay people have a latent desire to do, anyway. If that were to happen, would you expect the scientific community to drop whatever it was doing to go through all the old proofs of the heliocentric theory, just because some quack was making a lot of noise? You wouldn't, would you? But even if some member of the scientific community was so foolish as to waste his time on it, who would read his rebuttal? Not his fellow-scientists, or even intelligent laymen, because they already know the things he would put into his report and would have better things to do with their time than waste it rereading proofs that were firmly established centuries ago. And not the people who have become the disciples of the promoter of geocentrism, because they are the true-believer type and regard writings opposed to their master as heresy. That doesn't leave many interested people."

"But surely, Dr. Forest, that is a grossly exaggerated hypothetical situation?"

"Perhaps, Father. But look what happened several years ago when Erich Von Däniken initiated a spate of pseudoscientific books with his *Chariots of the Gods?* It and its imitators became immediate best sellers and made converts by the droves. The scientific community almost to a man gave Von Däniken and his ilk precisely the amount of attention they deserved—which was none at all—and the few who did respond were either ignored by the news media or were scorned for being narrow-minded apologists for the scientific establishment. People *want* to believe the irrational and the romantic, and they don't like being called back to earth by reasonable men. You are well acquainted with the attraction of the irrational, Father, since it is your stock in trade, what with burning bushes that talk, seas that part, walks on water, and the like. The emotional hold of mysterious things and forces that cannot be seen—whether they exist or not—has always been more powerful than mere empirical knowledge. And probably always will be, until and unless man evolves to a higher plane. In the meantime, it often seems that reasonable people are constantly fighting just to hold their own against unreasonable people and their ideas."

"I hope, Dr. Forest, that you are not equating the Christian faith with the belief that the earth was long ago visited by creatures from other planets, or such like."

"Of course not, Father. Religion is one thing, and promiscuous credulity is quite another. But they do have this in common—they both insist that their believers accept their particular 'truths' with no hard evidence whatever."

"True, but I would again insist that there is a difference between faith and credulity."

"Agreed, Father. But again we seem to have gotten sidetracked. I might wrap up this phase of the discussion with some general observations, then we can fall back and discuss the particulars as you wish.

"One of the cries most frequently heard from the Richardists is that if Richard were tried before a court today on the charge of murdering his nephews, or of having them murdered, he would be acquitted hands down because of the complete absence of any legally admissible evidence against him. It is an impressive point, but it makes the fundamental error of equating historical evidence with legal evidence. On the basis of the legally admissible evidence available to us today, we couldn't even convict Attila the Hun on a charge of disorderly conduct. It has never been a case of *legally* proving Richard's guilt, though if it were the evidence which the Richardists ignore would make a pretty telling case against him. All we can do is base our conclusions on the weight of the historical evidence available to us, and that evidence, despite a great many gaps and inconsistencies, makes it fairly certain that the responsibility for the boys' deaths rests not on Henry VII, as most Richardists would have it, but on Richard III himself."

With that I sat on the edge of my desk and let the class have at the question. Warren, naturally, led the attack, though he was supported by several others who remained bewitched by the romance of the Richardist position. From looks that Warren gave me as he scored debating points against his various classmates, I suspected that he was adhering to his position more out of cussedness than conviction. He was an intelligent, perhaps even brilliant, student, and I thought that the evening's session had probably taught him a valuable lesson which would stand him in good stead if he did pursue a career as an academic—that he should check and double check his facts and never rely too heavily on the work of others.

The discussion went on long after our usual ending time of nine-thirty, and several people were still arguing determinedly as I shooed them out of the classroom at a few minutes before ten. Warren held back until the others had left, then he walked out of the building with me without speaking. As I locked the door and turned to bid him good night, he said with a sheepish grin, "You sandbagged me, Dr. Forest."

"No, Mr. Warren. You did it to yourself."

He looked at me for a long moment then nodded his head slowly, a small smile on his lips. "I guess you're right," he said, and then, with a little wave of his hand, he walked off into the night.

Walking back to my apartment, I thought that Warren just might make it after all. It had been one of those nights that absolutely convince me that there is no more rewarding occupation on earth than teaching.

Part III
Solution

13

The next morning Ben telephoned my apartment just as I was leaving for the office and asked if I could meet him there in fifteen minutes. I agreed, then I asked, "What's it about, Ben? Did something break in the James-Tyrell case?"

"I'll tell you about it when I see you," he said shortly and hung up.

As I walked to the campus I puzzled over Ben's abrupt departure from class the night before. Of course, I knew that on occasion a policeman would have to miss class or leave in the middle of a session, but he had never before gotten up suddenly and rushed out with no explanation whatever.

I was no closer to understanding what had happened when I arrived at my office and found Ben leaning against the door. When we were comfortably settled inside, I asked him what was up.

He leaned forward in the stuffed chair, his arms on his knees and his hands clasped before him. "Monday morning," he began, "you tried to pump me for information on the James-Tyrell case and I cut you off abruptly. I was tired and frustrated, and besides, it was a confidential police matter and you didn't have any business with the information."

I nodded, uncertain of where he was headed.

"Well," he said, settling back in the chair, "now I'm going to answer your question. In fact, I'm going to tell you everything that I know."

"Why the sudden change of heart?" I asked.

"You'll see when I get through. This is going to take some time, John; do you think you could scare us up a couple of cups of coffee?"

I looked at my watch; it was a few minutes past nine. "Sure," I replied. "Marge usually has a pot brewed in the office by this time. Sit tight, and I'll get it. Cream or sugar?"

"Just black, thanks."

A few minutes later I was back behind my desk and we were taking small sips of steaming black coffee.

"I'll start from the beginning," Ben said, pulling a somewhat tattered copy of the Brookleigh *Ledger* from his pocket and tossing it on the desk in front of me. "Did you happen to see the news item I've circled there?"

The paper, which was more than two weeks old, was folded to an inside page, and a roughly drawn border of black ink encircled a short item headed PENSIONER SUFFOCATES. In a few sentences the story related how the body of John W. Dighton, eighty-three years old, had been discovered by his elderly housekeeper, a Mrs. Ripper, when she came to work as usual at eight o'clock in the morning. Cause of death was suffocation. The elderly Dighton, a retired postal worker who lived alone despite his advanced age, had apparently become entangled in his bedclothes and had suffocated in his sleep. There was no suggestion of foul play.

I couldn't for the life of me see how the accidental death of an ancient postman could have anything to do with Marian James-Tyrell's murder. I read it through again to see if I had missed anything; if I had, I was still missing it.

I handed the paper back, saying, "I may have seen it at the time, Ben, but if I did I've forgotten about it. What's your interest in this matter? It reads like a perfectly innocent accidental death."

"Yes," Ben agreed. "It does, doesn't it? Sergeant Williams took the call, and neither his report nor those of the technicians who went out afterwards indicated anything unusual. There were no signs of violence, aside from the disturbed bedclothes, and there was nothing about the state of the bedclothes to

124

indicate that Dighton had died by anyone else's hand. It looked as though he had just moved around in his sleep, gotten his head caught under the covers and his pillow, and suffocated to death without ever waking up. Given his age and his feeble condition, it's not very surprising. Hell, I didn't even go out on the Dighton call. There was no suggestion whatever that anything was other than the way it appeared." His tone was a mixture of belligerence and apology.

"What changed your mind?" I asked, guessing that he would not now be concerning himself with a simple case of accidental death.

"Well, the first hint that the death might not have been an accident came in the mail the next day." He rummaged in his pockets as he spoke. "We received an unsigned note—printed in block letters, of course—claiming that Dighton had been murdered to avenge two people named Richard and Edward." He found what he was looking for and handed me a piece of paper. "That's a photocopy of the note."

It didn't take long to read. It said:

> I HAVE DONE FOR DIGHTON,
> AS HE DID FOR RICHARD AND EDWARD.
> THE OTHER TWO SHALL DIE,
> THEN I'LL BE THROUGH.

I was not at my most brilliant that morning, and I did not immediately see the significance of the note. I handed it back to Ben, saying, "So this is what convinced you that Dighton had been murdered?"

"Actually," Ben said, shaking his head, "it didn't. You've got to understand, John, that there was absolutely no suggestion of foul play at Dighton's place. His death looked like an accident and nothing more. Sure, we double-checked after the note came, but it still looked like an accident. As for the note, it could have been written by some kook who had read about Dighton's death in the afternoon paper and wanted to get a little thrill out of confessing to murder."

He sighed and shook his head again before continuing. "So, no, the note didn't convince us that Dighton had been murdered. What convinced us was getting a similar note the day after Dr. James-Tyrell's death. You see, the newspaper article about Dighton's death had mentioned that he had been found with his head beneath his bedclothes, the victim of suffocation, and the person who wrote the Dighton note could have written it after the newspaper came out. But the note we got following the James-Tyrell killing came in the Wednesday mail—*before* we had released the details of her death. There was nothing about her death in the morning paper, and the note had to have been mailed before six a.m. for it to have been delivered in that day's mail. We figure that the killer must have mailed the note shortly after killing her." He handed me another paper. It read:

THAT'S DIGHTON AND TYRELL.
ONE MORE AND I'LL BE DONE.

I goggled at the note, then I blurted out, "Good Lord, man—you've had this second note for a week and you're only just now making the connection?"

Ben looked hurt, and I immediately regretted my tactlessness. Before I could apologize, he said:

"Listen, John. This is all old hat to you, a professor of British history, but to most folks, including us cops, Dighton and Tyrell and Edward and Richard are just names. The summer of 1483 was a long time ago."

"I'm sorry, Ben. Of course you are right. It's just that if you had told me about the notes immediately after Marian's death I could have made the connection right away. As it is, you've lost a full week."

He looked a bit worried. "Yeah. The lost time bothers me, too. It was twelve days between Dighton's murder and the James-Tyrell killing, and now James-Tyrell's been dead eight days. If this nut is on a regular schedule, he's due to strike again in four days' time."

"Yes," I said. "But now you know who his next victim is going to be." I pulled a telephone book out of a desk drawer and turned to the "F" listings. "Here we are. There's only one Miles Forest listed. At 419 Wesley Street."

Ben's worried look increased. "Yeah. And his phone number is 692-9168. But he's not answering it any more, because when he was staggering home from a bar last night he stepped out in front of a car and got his clock stopped. The driver kept going."

I whistled. "That doesn't fit at all. Do you have the driver of the car?"

"Not yet. We've got a vague description of the car from a

service station attendant who was about a block away, but it's not much to go on."

"But why would the killer switch methods with his third victim? It doesn't make sense."

"No, it doesn't, and I'm not at all sure that when we catch the hit-and-run driver we'll have the man who killed Dighton and James-Tyrell." Ben's brow remained creased with a frown.

"Well, either way, the killer should be through. Unless there's another Miles Forest around who's not listed in the telephone book, the killer's third victim is already dea—" I broke off in mid-sentence as I suddenly realized the cause of Ben's worried look.

He smiled grimly. "I wondered when it would dawn on you. What's your full name, John?"

All my life I had used the name John M. Forest. My bank account, my will, all the papers I had written were in that name. Like most people, I had a middle name, and I was luckier than some in that it wasn't something uneuphonious like Murgatroyd or Mudd. But I never had occasion to use it, and I always thought of myself as plain John M. Forest.

I tried to speak, but my throat was suddenly dry. I swallowed and then tried again. "As you apparently already know, it's John Miles Forest. But look, Ben. I never use that name. My phone is listed as John M. Forest, and this killer, whoever he is, has no way of knowing what the M stands for."

"Oh, he doesn't, does he?" Ben asked skeptically. "Look up Tyrell in that phone book."

I thumbed through to the last page of the "T" section. "There's a Tyrell, Barton, and a Tyrell, Wm. A. That's all."

Ben leaned forward. "You see what that means, don't you. This killer is out to kill three people. People who have the same names as the alleged killers of the princes in the Tower. John Dighton is in the phone book, but there is no James Tyrell. So what does the killer do? He searches until he finds one. And that one isn't easy to find, unless the killer is somehow associated with the college. If he can come up with a James-Tyrell, do you think he'll have all that much trouble finding out what that M in your name stands for?"

"It's not the same thing, Ben. Although she didn't have it in the phone book, Marian James-Tyrell went by that name on campus and probably elsewhere as well. So anyone could have found out her name. Middle initials are something else."

Ben looked skeptical. "Maybe. But if, as is quite possible, James-Tyrell's killer has some connection with this campus—here, after all, is where her name was most widely known—then he is in a better position than most people to find out more about you. At any rate, I'd be damned careful if I were you. Otherwise, you may end up rounding out the trio."

"Nonsense," I said, but my voice didn't carry much conviction.

"Let's back up a bit," I said, anxious to get onto another subject. "I take it that these notes have something to do with why you finally released Harrison Wednesday afternoon, but I'm not sure that I understand just what."

"Well, we know that the two notes were written by the same person. You will notice that, while block letters are used to keep from giving anything away about the killer's handwriting, some of the letters are printed the same in both notes. The enclosed parts of the R's, for example, are very small, making the letters look almost like inverted V's topped by small circles. And notice how the cross bars on the H's are all higher on the right than on the left. And, of course, the same features appear in the notes the newspaper received as well."

"The newspaper?" I asked. "You mean the *Ledger* received copies as well?"

"Yeah. Of both notes. They called when the first one arrived and asked us what it meant. The chief told them that it was just a crank note, and that there was nothing odd about Dighton's death. They decided not to mention it in the paper. When the second note arrived, I called the paper to see if they had gotten one too, and they had. I asked them not to mention it as it might jeopardize our investigation. They didn't seem too happy about it, but they've gone along with us so far."

"They?" I asked.

"Yeah," he replied. "That lady reporter you've been seeing lately and her editor, what's-his-name."

I nodded, realizing now that this was what Corinne had held out on me, then I said, "Okay, I see what you mean about the R's and the H's. But how does knowing that both notes were written by the same person help you eliminate Harrison as a suspect?"

"The deaths of John Dighton and Marian James-Tyrell are connected," Ben said, shifting to a more comfortable position in the chair. "We've known that ever since last Wednesday, though it wasn't until last night's class that I learned what the connection meant. If it weren't for this connection we would naturally regard James as our prime suspect. In fact, we *did* so regard him until the note showed up in the mail. Its arrival caused us to reorganize our thinking in several ways. First, the note was postmarked Wednesday and was delivered in the Wednesday mail. There is only one way that that could have happened—the note must have been mailed sometime between five o'clock Tuesday afternoon and six o'clock Wednesday morning at one of the mail boxes around town that have pickups three times a day—six in the morning, noon, and five in the afternoon."

"How on earth can you know that?" I asked.

"I checked with the Post Office, of course. There are three kinds of mail boxes: the kind I just mentioned, which are located in high-volume areas around town where there are concentrations of businesses and professional people; five-o'clock boxes, which are emptied once a day between five and six o'clock in the evening; and regular boxes, which are emptied by the mail carriers, usually between nine-thirty and noon, as they walk their morning routes. Mail is postmarked the day it is picked up, and local mail is generally delivered the next day. The only exception is mail picked up at six a.m., which is postmarked and delivered on the same day. Now, these six a.m. boxes are emptied at noon and at five p.m. as well, so any mail that is picked up at six in the morning *has* to have been mailed after five o'clock the preceding day. Therefore, we know for a certainty that the James-Tyrell note was mailed between those hours. Is that clear?" he asked me.

"Sure."

"Well, we know for certain that Harrison James could not have mailed that note before he left the rehearsal at 11:54—Steven Pollett, the director, wears a digital watch and he mentioned the time as everyone was leaving—or after my boys arrived at the house at 12:05, which leaves only an eleven-minute period in which he could have mailed it."

"What about earlier in the evening, before rehearsal?"

"That's out, too. Except for a couple of brief visits to the men's room, James was never out of sight of the other members of the cast from four o'clock on."

"All right. What about on his way home? He would have driven right past a box at the corner of Adams and Pine. Is that one of the six-o'clock boxes?"

"It is. But that box is in full view of the all-night service station across the street, and at that hour of the night the attendant would have noticed anything unusual—such as a man in a bright red Porsche hurrying to mail a letter—and he didn't. I've talked to him several times myself, and I believe him when he says no one mailed a letter there around midnight that night. He remembers the Porsche going past, but he says it never stopped.

"Besides, it was only nine minutes from the time he walked out of the theater building until he called the station. In those nine minutes he had a hell of a lot to do, especially if he killed his wife, without taking time out to stop and mail a letter. He had to get to his car in the parking lot, drive eight blocks to his house, put the car in the garage, enter the house, climb to the second floor, and telephone the police."

I started to ask a question, but he stopped me with an upraised palm. "There's something else," he said, "though it is anything but hard evidence. I just have a great deal of difficulty believing that the murderer would have mailed the note before he actually killed Dr. James-Tyrell. Suppose he mailed it beforehand and then something came up to prevent him from carrying out the murder that night. There'd be no way for him to call back the note, and its wording might give away the identity of the intended victim prematurely. Besides, the notes are obviously important to the killer, and I just can't believe he'd have taken a chance on blowing his plan by mailing the note before James-Tyrell was actually dead."

"I'm inclined to agree with you," I said. "Well, then, what about after he telephoned the station? Would Harrison have had time to mail the note after killing Marian?"

"How could he, with my men showing up two minutes after his call? And I know damned well he didn't mail it once that squad car arrived. He was under direct observation from that time onward.

"So you see the problem I had. Even if the physical evidence would allow for it—which it wouldn't—I didn't think it was psychologically possible for James to have mailed the note before killing his wife, and I didn't see how it was physically possible for him to have mailed it after she was dead. Therefore, when the note—which could only have been written by the killer, since he was the only person who knew about the murder before the six o'clock mail pickup—arrived, there wasn't anything I could do but let James go.

"Hell," he added, ruefully, "I'd have had to let him go in a day or two anyway, regardless of the postmark on the note."

"There was something else?"

"Yeah. I suppose I should have let him go as soon as the note arrived, but I was miffed, so I went after him about the Dighton killing. The note, whenever it was postmarked, connected the two killings, and I wanted to see if I could find a connection between James and the old mail carrier. Well, I was just wasting even more time. Dighton died sometime around midnight, Thursday the sixth. James said he had been in Washington until Friday morning of that week, and that his flight hadn't landed here in Brookleigh until two-thirty in the afternoon. I checked it out. He was there, all right—in Washington, I mean. And if he was there, he couldn't have killed Dighton here. So we let him go, finally."

He drained the last of his coffee and set the empty cup on the edge of my desk. Then he continued. "The second note, naturally, revived our interest in Dighton. His death had been handled routinely, and the reports were no more detailed than usual for an accidental death, so I sent the lab boys back out to see if they could come up with anything else. Unfortunately, the house-keeper, Mrs. Ripper, had given the place one last cleaning—for old times' sake, I suppose—and there was little to be found. They did discover that the back door of Dighton's house was warped in its frame and only took a little shove to open, even when it was locked, so that was probably how the killer got in and out without leaving any evidence of having done so.

"We checked into Dighton's background and found that he was a widower—for more than fifty years—with a single child, a daughter, now deceased as well. His only surviving blood relative was a grandson, Edward Vosik, who is an accountant in New York."

"Another Edward, eh?" I observed.

"Yeah, but we couldn't come up with a Richard. We tried to find some connection between Dighton and Marian James-Tyrell, but we had no luck there. Dighton and old man Tyrell had been members of the same lodge, but we've been unable to turn up any evidence that would suggest that they were more than nodding acquaintances. We've looked for Edwards and

Richards on James-Tyrell's side and found a handful of each — mostly distant cousins. And they haven't done us a damned bit of good." He sank back in the chair with a resigned shake of his head.

"Until last night I had completely struck out on trying to find a connection between the two victims. It seems that the two, and an unnamed third person, had in some way done something to two other people named Edward and Richard, which the killer was out to avenge. But last night's class shed a bright new light on the case.

"According to Sir Thomas More's account, three men — John Dighton, James Tyrell, and Miles Forest — were directly responsible for taking the lives of Edward V and his brother Richard at the orders of their uncle, Richard III. Now I have two corpses on my hands, a John Dighton and a James-Tyrell, together with notes declaring that they have been killed to avenge Edward and Richard and that there is a third killing yet to come, and frankly, John, I don't know what to do with it. This kind of crime hasn't come my way before, thank God, and it isn't covered in any of the standard texts. I need help, and that's why I've come to you. You know the people here on campus, you are as familiar as anyone else with the circumstances surrounding the crime — more familiar, now that I've filled you in — and you are the resident expert on Richard III."

"Whoa, there," I objected. "I'm not an expert on Richard III; my area of specialization is the nineteenth century, not the fifteenth. I have only a general knowledge of the period."

"Well, you're the closest thing to an expert that we've got around here, and I've got to work with what's available. First off, how many people are likely to know the details of the supposed murder of the princes — things like how they were killed and the names of their murderers?"

"That's an interesting point. As I said in class last night, most people don't bother to go to the original sources to form their opinions on the case. They usually just adopt someone else's opinion as their own. Shakespeare's, for example, or Josephine Tey's. But, as it happens, both Shakespeare and Tey name the three murderers. Tey gives their Christian names, but Shakespeare mentions only James Tyrell's, interestingly enough. And everyone in town had the opportunity to see *Richard the Third* last year. So I guess that I would have to say that anyone with more than a passing interest in the case would at least be familiar with the names of the murderers. And, if anything, the way the princes are supposed to have died is even more widely known."

"That's not much help, then." He thought for a moment. "Hell's bells, John, it just isn't reasonable to think that someone could get worked up enough to kill over something that happened hundreds of years ago."

"It may not be reasonable," I replied, "but it happens often enough. Look at the problems in Northern Ireland. Their roots go back for centuries. Why, the Statute of Drogheda, which effectively subjugated Ireland to the English Parliament, dates from the very period we are speaking of — it was passed in 1495. And the Protestant Orange Day celebrations in Northern Ireland commemorate an event that occurred three hundred years ago. As for the Richard III question, it generates harsh feelings even today. And it probably always will, since there is virtually no chance of any evidence being turned up which will be strong enough to convince Richard's supporters. Hell, most of those people are so fanatically devoted to the idea of Richard's innocence that a signed confession in Richard's own hand notarized by God Himself would not change their minds."

"I don't know about that, John. Some pretty responsible people call themselves Ricardians."

I grimaced at the use of the name the more pompous Richardists apply to themselves and cocked an eyebrow at Ben. He grinned.

"I've been doing some homework," he said.

"Okay. But look at how they became Richardists. The most fanatical have always divided the world into two diametrically opposed camps: those who believe Richard was a saint, and those who believe he was a monster. In their minds, there is no middle ground. Like most zealots, they present their case in a totally distorted manner, with no regard whatever for the niceties of historical objectivity, and they cram it down the throat of anyone who will listen. Professional historians, on the other hand, take the position that meaningful dialogue is impossible unless both sides are willing to give all the evidence a fair hearing, and they therefore prefer not to engage in debates with the Richardists, in the same way that reputable physicians will decline to enter into dialogues with quacks and charlatans. And, although it is a principal plank in the Richardist position that the historians have distorted the evidence, the fact is that the Richardists themselves are the distorters.

"Now," I said, warming to my subject, "since the Richardists are active proselytes and the historians generally speak only to themselves, is it any wonder that the Richardists are able to recruit large numbers of followers—even from among otherwise reasonable individuals?"

I was astride my hobby horse, riding at a full gallop, but Ben brought me to a halt. "That's an absolutely fascinating subject," he observed dryly, "but I don't think it's all that applicable to the problem at hand. You say these Richardists are fanatics with a disregard for the truth, and they no doubt have some equally kind words to say about you, but surely you are not suggesting that your average, run-of-the-mill Richardist is a homicidal maniac."

"Well," I admitted with a grin, "I suppose I wouldn't go quite that far."

A thought suddenly occurred to me. "You know, Ben, it's funny that the killer should have singled out Dighton, Tyrell, and (presumably) Forest and done nothing against the man who was supposed to have ordered the killing of the princes in the first place."

"You're right. That is odd. But maybe the killer just had too many Richards to choose from. After all, Richard is a fairly common name without a last name to hook it on to, and perhaps it made some kind of mad sense to him that since he couldn't kill all the Richards he ought to confine himself to Richard's instruments—the men who did the actual killing."

"Hmm. Maybe. Although Richard did have a last name after a fashion. But either way, Ben, it looks as though you are looking for someone who is quite mad. Hey—" I said as another thought occurred to me. "What if our madman identified himself with Richard?"

"I'm afraid you'll have to explain that to me."

"Well, suppose that this guy has for some reason gotten it into his head that *he* is Richard III—after all, if people can think they are Napoleon, why shouldn't they be able to think they are Richard III?—and he is feeling guilty about having his nephews put away. Maybe he is trying to assuage his own guilt feelings by killing off the people who did his bidding. Maybe he's crazy enough to transfer all of his guilt onto them and to think that killing them off will cleanse his conscience."

"That's pretty far out, John. And besides, it's not much help. People with that kind of mental aberration frequently appear to be perfectly normal in every other respect, and there's practically no way that we can find them out except to catch them in the act. In this case, that means catching the killer when he goes for his third victim—you, John."

"Forget it, Ben. I'm not being anybody's live bait. But you don't really mean that, do you?"

"Not completely, anyway. But look at the situation. We've gone over both murder scenes with fine-toothed combs, and we've turned up zilch in the way of useful evidence. Aside from this Richard III angle, we have no leads at all in the Dighton killing, and not the ghost of a motive, either. In the James-Tyrell case what evidence we have rules out the most likely suspect, her husband, and we're left with a handful of people who apparently had good reason to dislike her, but hardly enough reason to kill her. We're still looking, though, in both cases, and if there's a logical reason for these killings there's always a chance that good hard detective work will turn it up. But in this case the motive seems to be quite mad, and that kind of madness doesn't generally leave clues. I mean, if a person is known to be dangerously insane, he simply isn't allowed to run around loose, therefore the only clues as to who the killer is may be locked up in the killer's mind. If so, then four things may happen: he may confess; he may go completely off the deep end and give himself away; we may catch him in the act of killing his next victim; or we may never catch him at all."

Ben had extended a finger as he counted off each possibility, and he stared at the four digits as though he expected the correct one to identify itself. When it didn't, he continued.

"Given a choice, John, I'd rather be chasing a sane killer than a mad one. By the same token, you'd better hope that this killer isn't really mad; if he is, he's more of a danger to you than if he's sane, if only because we've got a better chance of catching him before he gets around to you if he is sane."

This talk was making me uncomfortable. "Come on, Ben," I said. "You're not really serious about me being the next victim, are you?"

"Dead serious, if you'll pardon the expression. This killer has said he's going to kill three people, and so far he's killed two of them. Odds are you are number three. If you don't get serious about it too, it will just be that much easier for him."

"Even assuming you are right, Ben, I don't see that I'm in any great danger. So far, he has killed an eighty-three-year-old man and a woman by suffocating them to death with their pillows.

The way they were killed seems to have been just as important to the killer as killing them—they were murdered in the same way that Richard's agents are alleged to have murdered the princes. If the method *is* important, then I don't have to worry about being run down in the street by a car the way my unfortunate and inebriated namesake was, or being shot, or having something heavy fall on me, or any other obvious method of accomplishing my death. I only have to worry about being suffocated with my bedclothes.

"Well, Ben, you've been in my apartment. You know that Herbie has the best security system money can buy for that building; there's no way anyone can get in there without a key, and I'll promise you that I won't lend my keys out to any madmen. But even if someone did manage to get into my apartment and catch me asleep in bed, I assure you that I wouldn't stay asleep long, once he tried to smother me. And he'd find me a damned sight stronger and harder to kill than an old man or a small woman."

"You through beating your chest?" Ben asked sarcastically. "Because if you are there are a few things I'd like to point out to you. First, even though his first two victims were smothered in their beds, we don't know that the killer is absolutely committed to that method. He may have regarded it as merely a nice touch, to be employed when possible but dispensed with if necessary. Second, your apartment is no more secure than thousands of others that are broken into every day. Do you have bars on your windows and doors? You don't, do you? Well, then, your apartment isn't break-in proof. Hell, it wouldn't be even if you had all those things. And third, I know you are in good condition—I ought to know, since beating you at racquetball is what keeps *me* in condition—but no one is at his physical peak when he is awakened from a deep sleep in the middle of the night. Besides, for all we know the killer could be a three-hundred-pound athlete you couldn't handle wide awake on your best day ever. This is a serious matter, John, and you'd better start taking it as such.

"Now, since I hope we have established your interest in the matter, is there anything else you can tell me that might give me a lead? About the Richard III angle or about Marian James-Tyrell?"

For the first time since I had returned from Everston I remembered the disturbance in my room at the Old South the night before my father's funeral. I had dismissed it as a simple attempted burglary, but in light of what Ben had just told me I now had second thoughts. When I told Ben what had happened his worried look returned in full force.

"You didn't report it to the police there?" he asked, somewhat annoyed.

"Hell, Ben, there was no reason to. There was nothing they could have done."

He thought for a moment. "Maybe not," he admitted. "But I think I'll do some checking all the same."

He got to his feet and stretched. "It might be a good idea, John, if you'd let me assign an officer to you twenty-four hours a day. For protection."

When I refused, he asked if I would be willing to stay with him and his family until things were straightened out. "I mean it, John," he said. "Millie and the kids would be delighted to have you."

"Thanks, but no thanks, Ben. I appreciate it; you know I do. But there really isn't any danger, and even if there were I'd have to learn to live with it eventually if this fellow is never caught, and the sooner I start working on it the better."

He argued with me for a while longer but finally gave up. "The offer will still be open, any time you want to take us up on it," he said, and then he was gone, leaving me to my nagging worries.

14

After Ben left, I spent the rest of the morning updating some lecture notes. Around noon Roger Wyndham emerged from his den next door and stuck his hairy, bespectacled face inside my door.

"You going to have lunch?" he asked. "Or is that pen you're chewing on going to hold you until supper time?"

We ate in the faculty dining room, where the food was inexpensive if uninspired, and talked desultorily about a wide variety of things, including Marian's murder.

We were returning our trays when I noticed Kate Roeder eating alone at a table near a window.

"I think I'll say hello to Kate," I told Roger as he used a napkin to rub a blotch of catchup into his tie, where it blended in nicely with earlier arrivals. "Want to come along?"

"Just a friendly 'Hello,' huh?" he replied, tossing the napkin after his tray, which was trundling off to the kitchen on a conveyor belt. "I'm sure this never occurred to you," he said, grinning, "but why don't you see if you can browbeat a confession out of her while you're at it?"

I didn't deny the insinuation. "You want to help? I'll even let you be the bad guy."

"You mean I'd get to push her around and make all sorts of threats and accusations—"

"—while I stand up for her, my teeth gleaming whitely and every hair in place, ready with a shoulder to cry on and an ear open for any unwary admissions which she might let slip in her relief at being saved from such a monster as you."

"Sounds like fun," he said, glancing at his watch, "but one of the campus cretins is due at my office any minute now, no doubt armed with a ingenious explanation for why he failed to show up for an exam last week, so I'll have to leave you to coerce whatever information you can out of her on your own. Be sure to let me know the results of your interrogation."

As Roger lumbered toward the exit I grabbed a cup of coffee and threaded my way across the room to Kate's table.

"Howdy," I said. "May I interrupt your solitude?"

She looked up from the papers she was glancing through as she grazed on a large bowl of salad. "John!" she exclaimed. Her rather plain face lit up with a warm and friendly smile. "Of course you may. Have a seat." From the alacrity with which she abandoned her reading I was certain that it must have consisted of student papers.

"Thanks," I said as I settled down opposite her. "How are things in the English Department?" I asked, plunging right in. "Have you been officially appointed chairman yet?"

Kate snorted. You wouldn't expect a matronly college professor to snort, but Kate often did, and the odd thing was that after the first time or two it didn't seem the least bit unusual. "Hardly," she replied. "I think they are holding off until the cops tell them whether I murdered Marian."

"Ah," I said, "so you are a suspect, are you?"

She looked at me shrewdly. "Don't pretend to be surprised, John. You're not a good enough actor. Of course I'm a suspect. That young Lieutenant Latta has had a suspicious eye on me ever since they let Harrison go."

"Yeah," I replied. "He asked me some questions about your relations with Marian. I'm afraid I had to tell him all about the chairmanship brouhaha."

"Don't worry about it." She waved my regrets away with a firm, young-looking hand. "It was common knowledge, and he probably got the same story from every person he talked to on campus."

"Not," I interrupted, "that any two of the stories would be exactly alike."

140

"No," she agreed, "but all of them would contain the essential information that there was no love lost between us."

"Sure, but, as I told Ben, people don't go around killing other people just because they don't like them."

"I don't know, John. There were times when I really did feel like murdering that woman. But I'd never kill anyone, not even Marian James-hyphen-Tyrell, just because she got a job I wanted."

"You wouldn't have another motive, would you, Kate?" It just came out. I hadn't intended to verbalize the thought, but sometimes the disconnect signal doesn't quite make it from my brain to my tongue.

For just a fleeting moment her strong face clouded and she emanated a strong aura of menace. Until that moment it had never seemed even remotely possible to me that Kate was capable, either physically or mentally, of hurting anyone. But right then I realized that, despite her age and her sex, Kate was a robust physical specimen, entirely capable of dropping from the roof outside Marian's window and running off into the night. And, what was more to the point, the look on her face effectively eliminated my doubts as to her mental capacity to do harm.

But the look was gone as soon as it came, and her voice was controlled when she replied. "I didn't kill her, John."

"Okay, okay," I said quickly, holding up my hands in a placating gesture. "I suppose you have an alibi for that night, anyway."

She snorted again. "I was where any self-respecting, fifty-eight year old widow should be at midnight — at home, in bed, alone. How's that for an alibi?"

"Not too hot," I admitted. "Well, if you didn't kill her and I didn't kill her, who did?"

"God knows," she said. "Considering who she was, the list of people with motives has got to be a yard long."

She leaned across the table toward me and, though there was no one within earshot, when she spoke it was with a lowered voice. "For my money, John, Harrison has got to lead the pack by several lengths. That he could have lived with that bitch for for as long as he did without killing her is one of God's major miracles. And if he did kill her, I'd say it was justifiable homicide at worst."

I considered telling her about the evidence which had cleared Harrison, but I thought better of it. Before I could respond, she brushed the topic aside with an abrupt gesture.

"Enough of this," she said. Her face softened, and the lines that had crept into it as we talked smoothed out. "I haven't had an opportunity to tell you before, but I was very sorry to hear about your father's death."

"Thanks, Kate," I said. "It's been a while now, and I'm beginning to get a handle on it." It wasn't a subject I felt like talking about just then, so I looked at my watch and said, "Well, I've got to get back to work."

As I pushed my chair back before rising, Kate placed a hand on my arm to stop me. Her grip was firm. She looked steadily into my eyes for several long moments, then she smiled sadly. "It's never easy losing someone you love, John," she said at last.

I covered her hand with mine and gave it a little squeeze. "No," I said, trying for a little smile, "I don't suppose it ever is."

I had lied to Kate. I was a long way from having a handle on my father's death. My mind had been busy all day and I had not once thought about him. I had, indeed, succeeded in blocking thoughts of him for some time, but all the while the pressure had been building up behind the dam I had constructed, and Kate's solicitude broke the dam and I was inundated with thoughts and memories of him.

After leaving Kate I started back to my office but I realized that my chances of solitude would be greater in the library, so I went there, secluded myself in my carrel, and tried to deal with the problem head on.

The root of it, I knew, was the distance between us, and I spent a long time mulling over the conversation with my cousin Jeff in my hotel room the night before my father's funeral.

"He really loved you, you know," Jeff had said.

I looked at him sharply from my perch on the ancient hotel bed. I knew that my father had taken Jeff under his wing after Jeff's dad died in a car crash nearly a decade before. He had, in fact, sold the big old house in which I had grown up and moved in with Aunt Mildred and her young son. Apparently Jeff had been more receptive to my father's overtures than I, because there was real feeling in his voice as he spoke.

I suppose it would have been natural for me to feel some jealousy, some resentment of Jeff for having been closer to my father than I had been myself, but what I felt as Jeff spoke was not jealousy but gratitude. I found that I was happy my father had at last found the kind of relationship I had been unable to give him, and I was glad Jeff had been able to share it with him.

"Yes, I suppose he did," I replied. "And I suppose I loved him, too. It's just that we were never much good at showing it."

Jeff surprised me by saying, "Yes, I know."

I looked at him again but didn't say anything. After a moment he went on.

"You more or less dropped out of the family when you went off to school, but I feel that I know you very well because of all my conversations with Uncle Richard. He talked about you a great deal, did you know that?"

I shook my head, thinking that I could imagine the things he had to say about his wrong-headed son.

"He did. He was immensely proud of you. You were still in graduate school when my father died, and that was when Uncle Richard started taking me hunting and fishing with him. While we were out on the lake he would talk to me about how you were learning to be a scholar and a teacher so that you could help other people to understand the world we live in. After you received your doctorate and began to publish, he would read to me from your articles—"

"He had some of my articles?" I interrupted, incredulous.

"He had all of them, and both books as well. At first I didn't understand what you were writing about, and I don't think that he did either. Not at first. But he checked books out of the library, or bought them if the library didn't have them, and before long he was explaining to me the background and significance of the matters you wrote about."

I was dumbfounded. In my boundless pride at having my first article published, I had sent my father a copy. He never acknowledged it, and I had not bothered to send him any of the others. To be honest, they were not the sort of thing that a non-specialist would like to read, and I certainly had not expected my father to keep up with my scholarly activities. There were, indeed, times when I was in danger of being bored by them myself.

"I never knew," I said at last. "Why didn't he say anything?"

"I couldn't understand that either, not for the longest time," Jeff said. He took a sip of his beer and then replaced it on the sturdy old end table beside his chair. "I asked him a time or two, but he never gave me a good answer. But I finally figured it out. He never said anything to you because he was just too proud himself to admit to you that he was proud of you."

"I'm afraid I don't follow you," I said.

"You understand, John, that most of what I know about your childhood I know through Uncle Richard. And Mother, of course. But I think Uncle Richard always tried to be completely honest with me, even when it caused him embarrassment. He didn't tell me this all at once; it just came out in countless conversations over the years.

"Well, Uncle Richard told me that when you were a little boy you were constantly asking questions about all sorts of things, from why we have the kind of government we do to why rabbits can't fly. He said that you didn't ask questions just to get attention, the way some kids do, but that you wanted the correct answer and you didn't stop looking until you got one you were satisfied with. Well, some questions don't have pat answers, and he said that when he would give you his opinion on one of these you would worry it like a dog will an old shoe."

He took another sip of beer, then he continued. "After a time he got tired of having his beliefs and prejudices challenged—I'm reading between the lines here, you understand—and he just stopped trying to answer your questions. Later, when he tried to interest you in the activities *he* was happy doing, *you* didn't respond, and he felt rejected again. It was, apparently, at this point that your relationship stopped developing. How am I doing so far?" he asked.

"Not badly. But what has all this got to do with his being too proud to let me know that he was interested in my work?"

"Everything, actually. Every man is different from every other man, and this is true for fathers and sons as well. Uncle Richard didn't realize this—or, rather, he didn't accept it—and he wanted you to be like him, to take up his interests and beliefs. When you didn't, he felt rejected, even betrayed, so he made no effort to share your interests or to understand your beliefs. It was a variation of the old if-you-aren't-for-me-you're-against-me idea.

"It wasn't until you had gone off to college that he began to realize that you couldn't be like him, that you had to be yourself and that he had to accept you for what you were, not what he'd like for you to be. Once he made that adjustment, you'd already begun to make a success of yourself, completing your graduate work and publishing in scholarly journals. When he accepted the fact that you were a son to be proud of, he had his problem half licked. Unfortunately, the other half of the problem was harder for him to deal with. To admit to himself that he was proud of you was one thing; to admit it to you was quite another. To do that, he would have had to admit that he had been wrong."

"Come on, Jeff," I interrupted. "That's nonsense."

"I know it is, but that's what he believed, nonetheless. He was just too proud to say to you that he should have encouraged you to become your own man, rather than giving up on you when you wouldn't become a carbon copy of him.

"You see, he saw himself as a failure as a father, and it galled him. When my father died, Uncle Richard saw me as a second chance, an opportunity to do right the things he had done wrong with you. Fortunately, I liked hunting and fishing, but even if I hadn't he would have made the necessary accommodations to share my life. So you might say that the fact that you and he had a less than ideal father-and-son relationship made it possible for me to have a wonderful father even though my own father had died.

"But, though he came to love me as a son, I never replaced you in his heart. You were always 'My son, John,' to him, and a large part of the bond between us was our mutual interest in you. He shared with me all the things he could remember about you, and together we pored over every word that you wrote, until we understood every point that you were trying to make."

He drank some more of his beer before adding, "I have for years thought of you more as a brother than a cousin."

I was shaken. This was too much to grasp at once, but I realized from listening to my young cousin reminisce that Jeff's loss was at least as great as mine. And realizing that made me conscious for the first time that I had indeed suffered a real loss. For years I had gone for long stretches without seeing or communicating with my father, and I had thought nothing of it. Now that the time for communication had passed, I began to think that there were a good many things that should have been said but now never would be.

It was late afternoon when I left the carrel and the library, but I was no closer to a resolution of my personal problems than I had been when I arrived.

15

On my way back to the apartment, I decided to stop in and speak to Herbie. I hadn't seen him since he'd left the Beefeater outside my door, and I wanted to thank him.

I climbed the four marble steps at the front of Palmer's Funeral Home and stepped into the recessed entrance. The front door was heavy and ornate, and the gilded glass in its upper half provided a clear view into the opulent foyer. My own front door, smaller and quite plain, was easily missed, as it was set into the wall perpendicular to and to the right of the main door. Beside my door were a mail slot, a buzzer, and an intercom grill. I used my key to enter and then walked a few feet down the narrow hall to the long flight of stairs which led to the second-floor landing. From there another flight doubled back to the third-floor landing outside my apartment.

At the top of the first flight I knocked and said loudly, "Herbie? It's John. You got a minute?" The unmarked door was Herbie's bolt-hole, which he used principally for avoiding casket salesmen and recently bereaved customers. It opened directly into his private office, where he spent most of his time.

After a few seconds the door opened and Herbie's face beamed out at me. "Come in, Johnny boy, come in," he said, opening the door wide.

Herbie's office looked more like a private study than a place of business. The walls were lined with beautifully crafted bookcases filled with books of all descriptions. I knew from numerous earlier perusals that they ranged from leather-bound sets to second-hand paperbacks and covered every topic imaginable, from science fiction to existential philosophy. More than once I had found books on those shelves which were unavailable at the college library or even through inter-library loan.

And Herbie's books weren't just for show. Having turned most of the duties of running the funeral home over to his employees—in particular to a morose, balding, fifty-year-old fellow that everyone, including Herbie, called Mr. Bill—it only took Herbie a couple of hours each day to make sure that everything was running profitably; the rest of his time he spent in his office, reading. He had been at it for more than twenty years, and he knew more about more different subjects than anyone I'd ever met.

Herbie was a true lover of knowledge. Everything in the universe interested him, and he was constantly poking his nose into something new. There was absolutely nothing that he wasn't interested in. Cesspools and supernovas, back-hoes and billiards, he read books on any and all subjects with equal avidity. He tended to concentrate on three or four topics at any one time, but they were constantly changing. He might be studying spiders one week and be neck deep in Spinoza the next, all the result of his letting his rampant curiosity lead him wherever it wished.

And his memory was phenomenal. He remembered not only facts, theories, and concepts with startling clarity, but also where he had come across them. He had once stumbled, somehow, across the abortive Polish revolution against Russia in 1830-1831, and when I mentioned that I was preparing a paper on British reactions to that revolution he was able to lend me several books on the subject which I not only did not have but didn't even know existed.

I told him once that he had a calling to be a scholar, but he disagreed. "Perhaps a scholar in the medieval sense," he replied, "but not as you probably mean it. I don't want to teach or write, John; I just want to learn. I'm a spectator, not a participant."

The business he had inherited from his uncle had given him the wherewithall to do as he pleased. He was one of the lucky ones, that tiny minority of human beings who manage to do precisely what they want to do with their lives. I didn't begrudge him his good fortune.

As Herbie led me across an expanse of deep carpeting to a pair of soft leather chairs on the far side of the office, I glanced at the titles of several books that were scattered on his desk.

"Witchcraft, Herbie?" I said to his back. "You haven't decided to start raising your clients instead of lowering them, have you?"

"Hell, no," he replied with a laugh, settling into the chair. "I'm making too much money in the lowering business to take a chance on rocking the boat. Actually, I was just following up on something that occurred to me while I was reading about the American military establishment." He paused deliberately, without further explanation.

He liked to tease me with these things, so I racked my brain and got lucky. "Military to Pentagon to pentacle to witches?" I ventured.

"Very good," he said, laughing his approval. If anything, he was more delighted when I was able to follow his tracks than when he lost me.

A cheerful outlook was so much a part of Herbie's personality that his face took on a faintly comic aspect on the rare occasion that he tried to look serious. That was a severe drawback for a mortician, so it was a good thing that he limited his involvement in the business as he did. "Er," he began, unpromisingly, "have you been making it okay?"

I didn't have to ask what he meant. "Yes, Herbie. Thanks. And thanks also for the bottle of snake oil. You'll have to come up and have a drop or two before it's all gone." In a few words I told him about the trip back to Everston and what I had learned about my father.

"Seems I completely misunderstood him, Herbie. Apparently I didn't even know my own father."

Herbie had listened to me talk with his accustomed attentiveness. Now he asked, "How does it make you feel? I mean, do you feel any different now that you've learned something unexpected about him?"

"Of course I feel different. I just don't yet understand exactly how. My father and I were never close. The funny thing is that I feel closer to him now that he's dead than I ever did when he was alive. Hell, I've *learned* more about him in the few days since his death than I did in all the years before he died. And I don't understand why he kept those things from me."

I explained what Jeff had said about my father's pride keeping the secret of his interest in me. "I suppose it could have been pride that kept the rest of it from me, too. But, damn it all, I wish I could have known all of this while he was alive. I wish I could have told him I was proud of him."

Herbie looked at me for a long moment. "Did you ever tell him you were proud of him? Or that you loved him? You mentioned once before that he was a master carpenter; did you ever say to him that you were proud of his abilities?"

"No," I replied guiltily. "I don't suppose I ever did. But I *was* proud of him, even if I didn't say it. And I did—do—love him, in a distant way."

"Maybe that's part of the problem—the distance. Apparently he loved you the same way. He was certainly proud of you, even though he didn't tell you. I think that's what you should hang on to—the fact that he loved you and was proud of you. Don't let the fact that he never said it bother you. And don't let the fact that you never told him of your pride and love bother you either. There's nothing you can do about it now. Besides, the important thing is that the feelings existed, even though neither of you managed to communicate them to the other."

"I suppose you're right," I said. Uncomfortable with the unexpectedly personal turn of the conversation, I steered it back to Marian's killing. Herbie had been, I knew, acquainted with Marian and Harrison socially, but he said he could think of no one who might want her dead. "Except, maybe, my cousin," he added with an impish grin.

"Your cousin?"

"Kate Roeder. Our mothers were sisters, you know."

I hadn't known, and I told him so, adding that I was surprised that anyone off-campus had ever heard of, much less remembered, Katie and Marian's run-in about the chairmanship.

"Oh, I don't mean that," Herbie said. "I knew about it, of course—Kate could talk about little else for the longest time— but that's not what I had in mind. I was thinking about the Elizabeth Barrett Browning letter."

I signaled my puzzlement with a raised eyebrow.

"Ah, you don't know about that, do you? From the way Kate ranted about it I assumed it was common knowledge all around campus. No? Well, let me be the first to enlighten you regarding the sordid details."

Herbie leaned back in his chair and steepled his fingers above his round middle as he gathered his thoughts. Then he began. "It all goes back to Walter Tilly, the oldest son of one of the founding fathers of the town of Brookleigh. Ever heard of him?"

"I can't say that I have," I admitted.

Herbie shook his head and muttered, "Such is fame. Actually, though, the fact that you haven't heard of him is quite central to the tale, as you will see shortly.

"Walter Tilly was a sickly child, and he grew up to be a sickly man. He had tuberculosis, or something of the sort, which kept him from engaging in strenuous activity of any kind. Not, of course, that he had any need to exert himself. His father was one of the richest landowners in the area, and Walter was waited on hand and foot throughout his relatively short life. He died in 1871, when he was thirty-four years old."

Herbie loved telling stories almost as much as he loved reading, and he was good at it. He was clearly enjoying himself.

"Though his life was short," he continued, "it was not without interest, for Walter was a poet. I suppose it was natural that so gentle and unstrenuous an activity as writing poetry should appeal to a semi-invalid like Walter, but probably his connection with the Barrett family had something to do with it as well. The American Tillys were distantly related to the English Barretts, and of course the most famous Barrett around at the time was Elizabeth, who, as everybody knows, married Robert Browning. It seems likely, therefore, that it was the example of his umpteenth cousin Elizabeth which spurred Walter on to become a poet, and he turned out quite a quantity of poems in his last twenty years. Enough, anyway, to rate a footnote or two in several studies of nineteenth-century American poetry. Of course, his fame was much greater locally than nationally, but we are now in an age in which poetry seems somehow alien and irrelevant to the great majority of people, and the light of Walter's fame has dimmed to near invisibility."

I interrupted to ask, "What has this to do with Katie, though?"

"Patience, Johnny, patience. My dear cousin Kate—her father

was a Tilly—is distantly related to Walter Tilly. She's not a direct descendant, as Walter never married, but she's a relative nonetheless, and over the past few years she has been working diligently on a literary biography of Walter Tilly which she hopes will revive his fame.

"As a relative, Kate had access to all the family papers, including several letters of little consequence from Elizabeth Barrett Browning herself. About the only thing of interest in these letters is Elizabeth's allusion on several occasions to an earlier letter, probably from the mid-1850s when Walter was first flexing his poetic muscles, in which she had apparently written extensively about her own views toward the art and practice of poetry. Search as she would, Kate never could locate the letter—or, for that matter, any correspondence whatever from August 1854 through June 1855. This was quite curious, because Walter was a meticulous record-keeper who kept copies of his own letters as well as the letters that others sent to him in careful, chronological files."

Herbie had me hooked and he knew it, so he paused at this point to ask if I'd like a cup of coffee.

"Hell, no, Herbie. Get on with it."

He smiled his cherubic smile, then he continued. "Well, last summer old Victoria Headley passed away. Her father was Roscoe Headley, a schoolmaster and would-be poet who died around the turn of the century. He was something of a Walter Tilly scholar himself and was doing some preliminary work toward a biography of Walter when he gained a small niche in the record books by becoming the first person in this state to be killed in a motorcar accident. He was walking home from school one day with his nose in a book and he walked right out in front of a Stanley Steamer travelling at full clip, though how he could have helped but hear the damned thing coming is a mystery to me.

"Anyway, old Roscoe had borrowed a great deal of material from the Tilly family, and after his death someone rounded up everything that could be found and returned it to the Tilly house. A few years later all of Tilly's papers were donated to Brookleigh College, which had just been established, and it was years before anyone looked at them closely enough to realize that there was a gap in the correspondence. By that time everyone had forgotten that Roscoe Headley had had the papers in his possession at the time of his death, and it wasn't until

Victoria's death last summer that the missing papers turned up.

"Victoria left her library and papers to the college, and they sat for several months in a storage room at the college library without anyone paying any attention to them. Kate, knowing of Roscoe's interest in Tilly, finally got around to looking through the several boxes of papers in hopes of finding something that pertained to Tilly, and she discovered that one of the boxes contained Walter Tilly's correspondence for the missing period. It had evidently been overlooked when the material was returned to the Tilly family following Roscoe's death, and it had been sitting over in the Headley attic gathering dust all this time.

"Naturally, Kate was delighted with the discovery, since it would enable her to flesh out that portion of her biography. But she was absolutely ecstatic when she got a look at the letter from Elizabeth Barrett Browning to young Tilly, who had written to his famous cousin asking many questions about the art he was attempting to master. It seems that Elizabeth answered at great length and made many significant observations along the way, and Kate was quite beside herself with the discovery."

Herbie sat up in his chair and leaned forward to put his elbows on his knees.

"Now you've got to remember, Johnny, that Kate is a dyed-in-the-wool Walter Tilly fan. She thinks he is a major American talent who has been ignored too long. When she found the letter she had an inspired idea about how she could get Walter some of the attention she was sure he deserved. She thought that all she needed to do was get people to notice Walter, then his talent would do the convincing for itself. And she intended to draw that attention to him by showcasing the Elizabeth Barrett Browning letter in her biography of Walter, showing how it influenced his later development. Elizabeth's fame is quite secure, and everyone of any importance whatever in the world of poetry would be sure to read a newly discovered commentary written by her. If that commentary was to be found in the middle of a biography of Tilly, Kate figured that many people would read about Tilly as well and his fame would soon spread.

"So Kate kept quiet about Elizabeth's letter and proceeded to incorporate it into her biography. She completed the manuscript last month and sent it off to her publisher."

Herbie paused for effect, then added: "And the very next

week Kate saw the letter printed in full in *Notes & Queries*. It had been contributed by Marian James-Tyrell."

"Good Lord!" I exclaimed.

"Precisely," Herbie replied, pleased with my response. "Kate was convinced that Marian's action had been deliberate sabotage—that she had sent the letter to *Notes & Queries* for the primary purpose of undermining Kate's book and her attempt to revive Tilly's reputation. It seemed more likely to me—and I told Kate so—that Marian had simply discovered the letter independently and, not knowing that Kate had any prior claim to it, had done what almost any other scholar would have done under the circumstances: rushed the significant discovery into print."

"Kate didn't buy that, huh?"

"Not a bit of it. In fact, she actually accused Marian of unethical conduct. Marian tried to explain, but Kate just wouldn't listen. She was convinced that Marian was deliberately trying to destroy her."

"But surely," I said, "Kate's publisher will go ahead with the publication of her book?"

"Yes, of course," Herbie agreed. "But now that the letter has appeared in print elsewhere, the chances of people reading Kate's biography in order to read the letter have dropped away to practically nothing. Kate was outraged as much for poor old Walter's sake as for her own, and she apparently allowed all her old hard feelings for Marian to fuel the fire when she faced her."

"When did the confrontation take place?" I asked.

"A couple of weeks before Marian was killed. It happened in Marian's office, and Kate says nobody overheard it, but Kate gets loud when she gets mad, and I wouldn't be a bit surprised if someone didn't hear at least part of it."

"I think you may be right," I said. "I've thought all along that Ben Latta was showing more interest in Kate than the old chairmanship dust-up warranted. If he's gotten wind of this, it would explain his interest."

"Maybe," Herbie said. "But if Kate was going to murder Marian, why would she wait two weeks to do it? It seems to me that she would be most inclined to do it immediately following her discovery of the *Notes & Queries* letter, while her blood was still hot."

I wondered for a moment whether I ought to tell Herbie

about the Richard III angle. I couldn't see any harm in it, so I explained about Dighton's death and the two notes.

When I finished, Herbie gave a long whistle.

"So," he said, "Latta probably figures that Kate hatched the vengeance scheme as a cover for killing Marian, right? Dighton was murdered around the time Kate found out what Marian had done. Kate killed Dighton, waited a while to give anyone who might have overheard the quarrel time to forget about it, and then knocked off Marian as well."

Herbie rubbed his hands together gleefully. "I like it, Johnny. I really like it. And I can see how Latta would like it as well."

I stared at him, startled. "My God, Herbie, you can't be happy that your cousin is a prime suspect in a murder case."

He looked a bit chastened, but only a little. "Of course I'm not, Johnny. I don't for a moment think that Kate killed Marian. Or Dighton either, for that matter. I was just thinking about how it was all tying together like a mystery story, with elements from five hundred years ago and a century ago weaving together with events of the present into a skein of intrigue and murder. Why, it's delightfully fascinating," he said, as animated as I had ever seen him.

He jumped to his feet and scurried over to the bookshelf behind my chair, where he plucked down a volume from high above his head, standing on his tiptoes to reach it. I could make out the title from where I sat; it was *A Study in Scarlet*. He started reading it as he walked back to his chair.

I had seen this happen a time or two before, so I knew it was useless to try to converse with him any further. I walked across to the door, opened it, and said, "See you later, Herbie," as I left. He waved a hand at me absently without taking his eyes from the page before him, and I closed the door behind me.

16

I must have been right at the shallowest point of a sleep curve, because all of a sudden my mind switched from a complete blank to alertness. There were no lingering memories of dreams and none of the mental sluggishness that results from being aroused from a deep sleep.

After coming upstairs to my apartment following my conversation with Herbie, I had caught up on some correspondence that had piled up over the past few weeks. I was hungry by the time I finished typing the last reply, but I didn't feel like going out for something to eat, so I popped a couple of frozen pot pies into the oven and showered while they were cooking.

Frozen pot pies aren't exactly *haute cuisine*, but they are easy to fix, and in my second bachelorhood I had developed a tolerance for them. I washed the pies down with a couple of beers and then settled down with one of the Hornblower books. I've been crazy about sturdy, dependable old Horatio since I was a kid, and every now and then, when I'm in the right mood, I pull one of them off the shelf and reread it.

All that fresh sea air made me conscious of being tucked inside an air-conditioned cocoon, so as I got ready for bed I opened a window and tested the air. It was cool enough, so I decided to sleep with the windows open. That had its drawbacks, since downtown Brookleigh was never entirely quiet at night, what with fools frequently cruising around at three o'clock in the morning with their windows down and their car radios set a notch or two above deafen, not to mention the occasional idiot who thinks his car isn't running right unless it leaves rubber at every curve and intersection. Still, there's something pleasant about sleeping in cool, fresh air, so I decided to bear with the fools and idiots for the night.

They had apparently decided to bedevil the residents of another part of town that night, and aside from an occasional tire squeal the night had been quiet. But something had awakened me. Without knowing why, I was certain it hadn't been a loud noise. Whatever it was had been quieter and closer at hand than the streets below. I lay there without moving and listened to the breeze rustle the curtains I had pulled aside when I opened the windows. No, that hadn't been the sound. My mind recognized the rustling for what it was and wouldn't have wakened me because of it.

Then I heard the noise again, a very soft, faint, squeaking sound.

To enable the air to circulate throughout the apartment, I had opened all the interior doors and all the windows. The sound came from outside my bedroom door, from the hall or possibly from the living room. It was a sound that didn't belong. I didn't own a dog or a cat or any other kind of pet that might make noises in the night, so there was no doubt in my mind that I had a visitor. The sound came again, and I recognized it at last.

My apartment had hardwood floors and I hadn't wanted to hide their beauty with carpeting, so I contented myself with a few throw rugs scattered about. For the most part the floor was bare, and wood floors, no matter how well-made they are, will always give a little, and in giving they sometimes emit little squeaks. What had awakened me were the sounds of someone walking very softly and very carefully across my floor.

I was lying on my right side, facing the doorway, with only a sheet covering me from the waist down. The moon was not out and very little light was coming in from outside. I could see the doorway without moving, but it was just a black rectangle in a slightly less black wall. Then I saw movement in the doorway.

Only the vaguest shape was discernable in the darkness. It moved forward slowly.

All of a sudden that morning's conversation with Ben came back to me in a rush: his warnings about looking out for myself, my rash assurance that no one could get into my apartment and catch me in bed. And there I lay, naked and defenseless, as someone stealthily approached my bed. I was terrified, and I cursed myself for not taking Ben up on his offer of a bodyguard.

I lay there without moving; I didn't know what else to do. If I made a move, the intruder would either attack me or flee from the apartment. There wasn't much chance of my catching him before he got outside, even if I was foolhardy enough to chase him. And if, instead of fleeing, he decided to attack, I would have lost the advantage of surprise before it could do me any good. So I decided to remain still until he was closer and then grab him before he could grab me.

He was very slow and very careful, making only those sounds on the floor which could not be avoided. At last, however, he reached the side of my bed and began to lean over me.

At that instant I brought up my left arm, which had been lying on my side, as hard and as fast as I could, slamming it into the intruder's head. The nerves in my forearm screamed their displeasure, but the gratifying sound of the intruder's head bouncing off the headboard made the pain easier to bear. I rolled out of bed before he could grab me, only to find that he was past grabbing anyone for the moment. He had collapsed on the pillow where my head had been, apparently knocked unconscious by my unexpected attack. Of course, I thought, he could just be faking it, hoping to turn the tables on me and take me by surprise as I had done him, so I didn't reach across his body to turn on the bedstand light. Instead, keeping an eye on the still form all the time, I walked over to the overhead-light switch beside the door and flipped it on.

It was a woman, I saw with surprise. She was lying face down, half on and half off the bed. I walked across to the bed and carefully turned her over. It was Corinne! I sat down on the bed beside her to consider the situation.

Corinne had certainly had some strong feelings against me, but I would not have thought they were strong enough to make her want to kill me—especially not in such a way as to cause two other people to die as well. Fate hath no fury like a woman scorned, the saying goes, but she wasn't the one scorned—she was the one doing the scorning. Besides, we seemed to be getting back to normal after our falling out. Why should she want to kill me now? Unless, of course, she had only been pretending to want us to get back together again.

I looked down at her and said aloud, "Why, Corinne?"

She was still unconscious. It occurred to me belatedly that I hadn't checked to see if she was still breathing. Hurriedly, I bent down to her and felt her sweet breath on my face. I put my fingers on an artery in her neck and felt a strong, steady pulse. She looked as though she might slide off onto the floor at any minute, so I picked her up and put her squarely on the bed. Then I slipped into a pair of pants and a T-shirt before sitting in a chair and thinking.

I looked over at her after a time and noticed something that I should have seen before. I kept both pillows on the bed, though I only slept on one. The other lay more or less in place throughout the night and made the bed look more symmetrical in the daytime, so I left it there. It was still there in its accustomed place, slightly rumpled from having been fallen upon by an unconscious body, but still there. Thinking back to the moment before I had lashed out with my arm, I couldn't remember seeing her pick up the pillow. It was dark, of course, but I would have seen or felt it if she had moved the pillow, and I had seen and felt nothing. I looked around the bed for something else that she could have used to smother me, but there was nothing, not even her purse. I walked out into the hall and looked into the living room. In the light that spilled from the bedroom I could see her purse lying on the couch with her shoes on the floor beside it.

Feeling guilty and a bit embarrassed, I went back to the bedroom to check on Corinne. She had a large knot above her left temple where it had struck the headboard. When I touched it lightly she groaned and opened her eyes. They didn't focus at first, then they turned and fastened on my face.

"John?" she said, her voice full of question.

I barely made it to school in time for my nine o'clock class the next morning. I had brought Corinne a couple of aspirin for her headache and then had sat on the bed beside her while we

160

talked. She explained that she had been out late covering a warehouse fire, and on her way home she had decided on a whim to stop by my apartment and say hello. Though it was not much past midnight, she could see from the street that my lights were out, but she still had a key to my place from happier times, and she decided to come in quietly and surprise me.

"It was a stupid, childish thing to do," she said, "but I just wanted to see you."

I smiled at her and tousled her hair, which brought a wince to her face when my hand brushed her bruise. That produced another round of apologies on my part, and my efforts to comfort her nearly got out of hand. Before that could happen, she pushed me away gently and swung her feet to the floor.

"I can't stay, John. Really. I've got to be up early in the morning to write a couple of stories. Besides," she added with a crooked grin, "I've got this splitting headache."

I laughed at that and then accompanied her downstairs to her car, which was parked just outside. When she was seated behind the wheel, I leaned in the open window and kissed her gently on the cheek.

"How about dinner tomorrow night?" I asked. "We could splurge and have lobster at the Gloucester House."

"I can't tomorrow night, John. I've got to cover a meeting of the planning commission at six-thirty, and God only knows when those windy bastards will get tired of the sound of their own voices and decide to call it a night. How about Saturday night, instead?"

"Fine," I said, and I kissed her again—this time not on the cheek—before she drove off.

Back in the apartment I locked the door, putting the chain bolt on this time, and went back to bed. But not, for the longest time, back to sleep. My body wanted to sleep, but my mind was wide awake. I lay there in the cool darkness as thoughts of Corinne competed for my attention with thoughts of a murderer who was still at large and who might at that moment be plotting my death. Thoughts of my father also surfaced at odd moments, and just before I managed to get back to sleep I felt a very intense, very impossible need to talk to him about my life.

What with all that, I slept right through my alarm and had to forego my morning coffee in order to make it to class. Afterwards, I stopped by to pick up a cup of Marge's coffee and took it back to my office. I was upending the cup to get the last drop when

Riddle, the administrator with whom Marian had been at odds, showed up.

I never cared much for Glen Riddle, though I admit that my antipathy for him had professional rather than personal roots. As a person, he might have been the nicest guy since Captain Kangaroo, but I only knew him in his professional capacity, in which he represented most of the things that I thought were wrong with our system of higher education.

Colleges and universities had developed as havens for scholars, and originally no one who was not a scholar, either a teacher or a student, was involved in their operation. They existed solely for the purpose of preserving, perpetuating, and increasing human knowledge. As they grew in size and complexity, their interaction with the outside world increased, and it became necessary for some strictly non-academic functions to be performed. In the beginning, these functions were carried out by the scholars themselves, as onerous but necessary duties. In time, as these responsibilities increased, it became necessary for some of them to spend more and more time away from their academic pursuits, tending to the day-to-day details of running the institution. In a way this was a waste, for the time a scholar spent on mundane matters was time he couldn't spend increasing his own and others' knowledge, but it had the advantage of ensuring that non-academic decisions regarding the administration were made by individuals whose roots were in academia — in other words, the institutions continued to be run by and for scholars.

In more modern times, however, this has begun to change. Tremendous increases in both the size of colleges and the degree of their interaction with the outside world have created a need for full-time administrators, individuals whose exclusive interest is in the administrative side of running a college. This has freed the scholars to return to their academic activities full time, but it has left control of affairs of the college in the hands of non-academics. The new breed of administrators are not physicists and philosophers and historians, but businessmen who see the college in terms of profit and loss. They are concerned not with turning out educated individuals better able to understand, deal with, and improve the world, but with increasing enrollments, improving the college's physical facilities, building new football stadiums, and the like. They have industrialized higher education, turning colleges into factories which take in raw material in the form of high school graduates, run them through various manufacturing processes, and then, after four years, grind them out as shiny new college graduates.

Nowadays, the new breed of administrators are mostly salesmen. They have a product to sell to the students, and they have a product to sell to those who contribute financial support to their institution. They are businessmen, and their aim is to turn higher education into a business. And the greatest tragedy of all is that they are succeeding.

Glen Riddle was one of this new breed. He had gone through the system himself, taking such courses as would fit him to run a college as a business, and he had acquired little understanding of or sympathy for traditional educational values. It was, in fact, his contempt for those values which led to his run-in with Marian James-Tyrell.

Riddle's desire to increase Brookleigh's enrollment and income by waiving admissions requirements for minority students with deficient backgrounds would have particularly taxed the English department. Marian had argued with all her considerable wit (and a little help from me) that providing remedial assistance for these students was asinine without additional funding for specialized instructors. The administration's tacit alternative of simply lowering standards was unthinkable, so in the end the program had been neither rejected nor implemented. The open-door admissions policy had been Riddle's pet project, and its defeat was one of the few reversals he had met in his meteoric career.

Riddle, however, had apparently emerged from his defeat without a scratch, and all indications were that he still enjoyed President Wilkerson's full confidence. I occasionally saw him striding purposefully across campus, a leather envelope tucked under his arm, the very picture of efficiency on the rise. His boyishly handsome round face was usually graced by a small smile that came just a hair short of being smug. Of middle height and a slight build, he was disposed to dark, tailored suits and Republican haircuts.

He had no more reason to like me than I had to like him. I had made no secret of my belief that the administration was the least important element of the college community, coming in a distant third begind the student body and the faculty. In common with most administrators I had encountered, he tended to hold just the opposite view — that students and faculty existed solely

163

to give the administration something to administer. The gap between the lions and the Christians was nothing compared to the gap between us. I was, therefore, quite surprised to find him knocking on my office door shortly after ten o'clock that Friday morning.

"Come in, Glen," I said. "Have a seat."

He closed the door carefully behind him and looked dubiously at the ragged stuffed chair. There being nowhere else to sit, he finally settled himself into it, and a brief look of surprise passed over his face when he realized that the chair made up in comfort for what it lacked in looks.

I stared at him without speaking as he sat there trying to decide how to start. He was having such a time of it that I finally relented and asked, "What can I do for you, Glen?"

He shifted nervously in the chair.

"Well, John," he said at last, "I believe you are friends with this Lieutenant Latta who is investigating Marian James-Tyrell's death."

"That's right. Ben's a friend as well as a student of mine."

"I see. That's what I thought. Well, I wonder if I might impose upon our acquaintanceship to ask you to serve as an intermediary between the lieutenant and me."

"I don't understand."

"Well, it's damned embarrassing, actually, but Latta has been asking some personal and, well, embarrassing questions of our friends—that is, my and my wife's friends—and the questions are beginning to get back to Joannie and disturb her."

"Damn it, Glen," I said, "Latta is conducting a murder investigation. He's got to ask questions to find the killer, and that's a damned sight more important than a few hurt feelings. Besides, what makes you think that I could have any influence over how Ben performs his job?"

"You misunderstand, John. I'm not asking that you try to get him to stop asking questions. I'd like you to arrange for him to listen to some answers."

"You've lost me there. I'm sure he'll be overjoyed to listen to any answers you want to give him, quite without my intervention."

"Yes, yes, I know that," Riddle said, impatiently. "I'd just like to know that he will treat the answers I give him with some discretion. Talk to him for me, John, and get some sort of assurance from him that what I have to say won't be broadcast all over campus and all over town the next day."

"Hell, Glen, you can trust Ben. He's honest and he's discreet. He won't pass along any information that isn't germane to the case."

Riddle didn't give up. "He's your friend, John, so naturally you'd think that about him. I don't know him, and from the little I've seen of him I'm inclined to doubt that he'd bend over backward to keep my secrets for me. If you ask him, though, and he says he will, then he'll be more inclined to keep his word."

"Well, of course I'll ask him, Glen. But you have nothing to worry about from Ben."

"Thanks, John. And one more favor: would you sit in with us while I talk to him? You know, as a sort of witness?"

"Of course, if you want me to. And if Ben will permit it."

"He'll permit it," Riddle said, in a rather weak show of defiance, "or I won't talk."

"All right. We'll see. When do you want to see him?"

"Right away. Now, if it's possible—that is, if you don't have a class . . . ?"

"No," I assured him. "I'm free until two o'clock. Let me see if I can find him."

Ben was in his office, and he was surprised and pleased with what I had to tell him—at least until I got to the part about Glen wanting me to sit in on the interview.

"He means it, Ben," I said into the phone. I looked across at Riddle, who nodded his head vigorously. "He won't talk unless I'm there."

"God damn it to bloody hell!" Ben all but shouted into the phone. "In more than a decade on the force I've never encountered such a lot of goddamned prima donnas! I suppose he wants to name the place, too?"

"Just a second," I said, then covered the mouthpiece with my hand. I asked Riddle, "Where do you want to meet him?"

"Is your office all right?"

I uncovered the mouthpiece. "How about my office, Ben? In about ten minutes?"

Ben mouthed off some more, but it was mostly for show; he was getting what he wanted, and a trip across town was a small enough price to pay for it.

While we waited for him to arrive, I went down the hall to a

165

conference room and brought back a wooden captain's chair. I put it out of the way in a corner of my small office and was sitting in it when Ben arrived a few minutes later. He saw what I had done and gave me a nod as he went around and sat down at my desk.

He hadn't bothered to shake hands with Riddle, and he started in on him without preamble.

"All right, Dr. Riddle, what is it that you've finally decided to tell me?"

Riddle had been uncomfortable just talking to me, and he seemed positively mortified now that Ben was there. He cleared his throat noisily.

"I would like to have your assurance, Lieutenant Latta, that you will not make public anything that I tell you unless it has a direct bearing on Marian James-Tyrell's murder."

"Bullshit, Riddle. You had your chance to give me some straight answers a week ago; don't start making any demands on me now. But if it'll make you feel any better, I'll tell you that all I am interested in is solving this case before anyone else gets hurt"—he shot me a quick glance. "I'm not going to air any of your dirty laundry unnecessarily. Now what is it that you've got to say? I take it that you are going to change your story about having had no contact with Marian James-Tyrell since that run-in during a faculty meeting last year?"

"You've got it all wrong, Lieutenant," Riddle replied, "and the questions you keep asking around are making a wreck of my personal life as well as my professional life. Dr. Wilkerson tries to act as though nothing's changed, but even he has begun to behave more distantly toward me, and last night I caught my own wife looking at me with something like fear. I saw her in a mirror when she didn't know I was looking. The longer you keep at it, the worse it gets. So I've decided to tell you the truth in hopes that you'll leave me alone and let me get on with my life."

"All right, Dr. Riddle. What is the truth?"

Riddle bit his lower lip as he looked from Ben, to me, then back to Ben again. He hesitated for a moment longer, then he said in a flat voice, "Marian and I were lovers."

"Jesus Christ!" I exclaimed, before a quick, hard glance from Ben shut me up. If Glen Riddle thought he was getting himself off the hook by that admission, he was a lot more stupid than I would have imagined. But he wasn't through.

"It's a long story, and it's still not what you think. After the dust-up over the open-admissions policy, Marian and I detested each other. Or at least we thought we did. But sometimes feelings like that are actually camouflage for real feelings of exactly the opposite sort. That was the case with us. We felt a powerful mutual attraction, and we denied it by acting as though what we were feeling was repulsion.

"It didn't take long for us to come to grips with our true feelings. After that faculty meeting I went to Marian's office to try one last time to impress upon her the importance of opening the college's doors as wide as possible. She didn't agree with me—she never did, not even after we became involved—but she was noticeably less hostile than in the meeting. I found myself, unaccountably, blushing in her presence, realizing for the first time just how attractive a woman she really was. She told me later that she had had the same experience—"

He broke off momentarily, then he said, "The details don't matter. All you need to know is that we soon became lovers. And not just in the physical sense," he added, defensively. "Marian was a very sensuous woman, I know that, and I know that she had several affairs before me. But this was different. What we had was really love. As for me, I had been faithful to Joannie until Marian. Our marriage was a fairly good one, of the unspectacular type. But what I felt for Joannie paled to insignificance beside what I felt for Marian.

"And I know that Marian felt the same, because she wanted to marry me. Almost from the beginning she talked about it. Her marriage to Harrison was completely devoid of warmth, and her affairs with others had been devoid of love. Together, she and I had a perfect relationship. But we were both married. She wanted us both to get divorces right away, but I knew that if I did, it would ruin my chances of taking over as president when Dr. Wilkerson retires.

"I told her that we would have to be discreet, that we must keep our affair secret until we were both free, and then wait a respectable period before we married. And she loved me so much that she agreed. She was going to go ahead with her divorce first, and I was to follow several months later.

"And then she was murdered. I was shattered, but of course I couldn't show it. No one knew about us, and with Marian dead I wanted to make sure that no one ever did. I had no reason to go through with my divorce once Marian was gone. Joannie has been a good wife, and of course there are the kids.

"So can you wonder why I didn't tell you all this when you

first asked? I wouldn't be telling you now, except that the problems you are causing with your constant questions and insinuations are as bad as the ones I hoped to avoid by remaining silent."

He leaned toward Ben and said beseechingly, "I didn't kill her, Lieutenant. I couldn't! I loved her. And the fact that I want to preserve my marriage now that she's dead doesn't mean that I didn't love her. Why should I throw away my marriage and career now, when it can do no good?"

I liked Riddle even less after that exhibition, and from Ben's behavior I could see that he had been similarly affected. He went over the story in detail, demanding dates and places, and when he was through he told Riddle that he'd keep the information to himself unless there were some pressing need to do otherwise.

When the administrator was gone, Ben snorted and shook his head. He looked over at me and said, "You know that bastard; what do you think?"

"I really don't know him well at all," I said, "but I'm inclined to believe him. There's nothing in what he said that wouldn't fit in with what we know. Instead of Marian being the person who spread the rumor about Riddle having an affair with a married woman, Marian was herself the married woman in question. I'll buy that. I always said that rumor mongering wasn't Marian's style. And, frankly, I don't see how he has helped himself by spilling all this to you, unless he did it for the very reason he said—to keep the damage to his personal and professional lives to a minimum by telling you the truth in hopes of getting you off his back."

"Maybe," Ben said ambiguously. "But I'm going to check his story damned close before I accept it. He's a slimy sort of fellow."

"Assuming it all checks out, where does this leave you?" I asked.

"In a real bind," he replied. "The chief is on me for some action, and if I don't arrest somebody soon he's hinted that he'll assign the case to someone else."

"Ouch," I said.

"My sentiments, exactly."

"So what are you going to do?"

"Well, if something doesn't turn up soon I guess I'll have to haul in the Phillips kid and squeeze him a bit. Right now, he's the most likely of a pretty unsatisfactory bunch of suspects."

"Do you really think he did it?" I asked.

"Hell, John, I don't know. But I've got more on him than I do on anyone else."

"Which isn't much," I interjected, unhelpfully.

"Which isn't much," he repeated. "But look. He had opportunity—his fraternity house has almost as many doors as it has windows, so getting in and out unobserved would be a piece of cake for him. And that roommate of his appears to be a junior-grade alcoholic; he's drunk more nights than he isn't, and nobody would know that better than Phillips."

"Hmm," I murmured. "I didn't know the roommate was such a boozer."

"Well he is. And wouldn't you know that he was out cold on the night Dighton died, too. Phillips claims he was in his room all night, studying, but he can't produce a single soul who saw him."

"What about the other suspects?" I asked. "I mean, do they have alibis for the night of Dighton's death?"

Ben grimaced. "They all do, at least for part of the night. But the time spread on the Dighton death was so great that any of them could have gotten away long enough to kill him. Besides, we didn't start asking questions about Dighton's death until several weeks later, by which time all of my prize suspects were pretty hazy about what they had been doing that night and when they had been doing it. All of them, that is, except Phillips, who has a story but can't back it up. Even his girlfriend can't alibi him; she says she wanted to go to a show but he insisted that he had to do some extra reading for one of his courses. They had a bit of a fight about it, as a matter of fact."

"Quite a devoted student, is our young Phillips," I remarked. Ben ignored my interruption.

"As for motive," he said, "jealousy is about as good a motive as you can come by, nowadays. Phillips was spurned by Marian James-Tyrell after a dogged pursuit of several years, and that must have smarted. With what we just learned from Riddle, we now know that she and Riddle took up with each other sometime after she got rid of Phillips. Somehow, Phillips might have found out about them, and he is as likely a source as any for the rumor that Riddle complained about. Even if he didn't start it,

169

he probably heard it and was able to figure out who the woman was. Either way, it strengthens Phillips' motive."

"Still—" I began, but Ben anticipated me.

"Still weak, I know. But how about the Richard III angle? My recollection of Wednesday night's class meeting is that Phillips was suspiciously knowledgeable about the details of the deaths of the princes."

"So was Warren," I said.

"Yeah," Ben replied, getting to his feet and preparing to leave. "But I'd give long odds that Warren and James-Tyrell were never lovers."

"You've got a point there," I admitted.

He paused in the doorway. "Are you watching out for yourself?" he asked me. "Locking up tight at nights and all that?"

"Yes, Mother," I replied sarcastically, omitting to tell him about last night's episode.

"Seriously, John, be careful. Are you sure you won't reconsider and come stay with us? Or at least let me assign you a bodyguard?"

For an instant, remembering those terrifying moments in my bedroom, I was tempted to take him up on the bodyguard. But I had learned my lesson and would be careful. "No, thanks, Ben. I'll get along fine by myself."

He shook his head in resignation, then he left with a brief wave of the hand.

17

fter my last class Friday I returned to my office and updated my lecture notes for the following week's classes. I normally try to stay a couple of weeks ahead, but things hadn't been normal for some time.

It was early evening before I walked up the front steps of Palmer's Funeral Home and through my little door. I picked up my mail and carried it upstairs without looking at it.

I grabbed a beer out of the refrigerator and took it back to the living room. Switching on a lamp at one end of the couch, I sat down and went through the mail.

It was the usual assortment, but one large brown envelope caught my eye. In the upper left-hand corner was imprinted HARLEY WILSON, ATTORNEY AT LAW, and beneath it was an Everston address. Wilson, I knew, had been my father's lawyer. The outer envelope contained only a plain white number-ten envelope, on the front of which was penned my name in my father's handwriting. My fingers trembled slightly as I gently opened the flap, trying not to tear the paper any more than necessary.

Inside were several sheets written in my father's unique writing, a curiously elegant blend of printing and script. For a

few minutes I just held the pages. Then I unfolded them. At the
top of the first page was a date about four months earlier, and
the salutation:

My Dear Son John,

*I've just returned from a visit with old Dr. Timms—you
remember him, he set your arm when you broke it falling
out of the pecan tree behind the old house—and he has
confirmed what I've suspected for some time now. My heart
is giving out. I've had a few mild attacks over the past year
that I haven't told anybody about, but the one this morning
was the worst yet, and old Doc tells me that I don't have
much time left. Six months at the outside, he said.*

Six months.

*There was a time when that news would have driven
me wild, made me rant and scream at the injustice of it.
But, to my considerable surprise, I find that I can accept
it with scarcely a qualm. Six months can be quite a length
of time, and I have nothing important left that needs doing.
Or only one thing, this letter, and it will be finished before
this evening is gone. Then all I'll have to do is wait, and
while I'm waiting I'll just go on the way I have for many
years.*

*Looking back over my life—and nearly six decades is
not a bad life, although it is a bit short of the Biblical
standard—there are only two things that I really regret:
that your mother was taken from me so soon, and that I
wasn't a better father to you. The first wasn't my fault, but
the second was, and I regret it all the more for that reason.*

*I love you, son. I can't remember when I last told you
that—way back when you were too young to remember,
I suppose—but I do love you. But I let two flaws in my
personality keep me from showing it. I was an arrogant
man when you were a child, and you kept stepping on my
pride. I didn't learn to bend until it was too late. You grew
up proud and arrogant yourself, and that only made things
more difficult.*

*And then one day, after you'd gone off to college, I looked
around me and took stock of my life. What it came to,
putting aside the material things, was that I had my pride
and my arrogance, and that was about it. My wife was
dead, my son was a stranger, and my friends—to tell the
truth, I wasn't rightly sure that I had any friends, really.*

*Well, it wasn't easy, but I set about trying to see if I
couldn't make my life amount to more than that. I had
to ease up on feeling superior to people, but I found that*

*there were plenty of them out there who were willing to
meet me more than half way at being friends.*

*These last years have been good years for me, son, filled
with the joy of having friends and the even greater joy of
being one. The only thing I couldn't change was the past.
When you were growing up, I had a chance to be a good
father to you, to give you the support and the
understanding and the love that every child has a right to
expect from his parents. But I failed to give it to you. I
didn't even realize that I had failed until you were already
grown, and by then there was nothing I could do.*

*I have wanted your love all these years, son, but I've
known all along that when I had a chance to earn it I
didn't take it. And how could I go to you, once you were
grown, and say that I wanted your love as a father? So I
left it alone. I've followed your career, son. I've kept a closer
eye on you than you know. And you've done a lot to make
me proud of you. But one thing I've noticed, even from
this distance, is that you've still got maybe a bit too much
pride and arrogance yourself. I don't say that to belittle you,
son. I mention it only because I know what a terrible price
it can exact, and I don't want you to ever have to pay it.*

*This letter has three purposes. To tell you that I love
you and I'm proud of you. To beg your forgiveness for
having failed you as a father. And to caution you ever so
gently against letting your pride and arrogance get the upper
hand.*

*I won't mail this letter to you while I'm living. I'll leave
it with Harley Wilson and instruct him to mail it to you
a week or so after I'm dead. I wish I had the right to tell
you these things face-to-face before I die, but I forfeited
that right long ago. Still, I want you to know that if I had
it to do over again, I'd make you the best father that any
boy ever had.*

Forgive me, John. I love you.
Dad.

I sat there staring at the last page until the words began to
blur and I realized that I was crying. At first it was only tears,
but soon the sobs came. Great, tearing sobs that went on and
on. I had not cried like that since my mother died when I was
five years old.

Finally, ages later, the sobbing stopped. Another age passed,
then I went into the bathroom and washed my face. The eyes
that looked back at me in the mirror were swollen and red.

I couldn't bear to think about it any more that night. Tomorrow would be soon enough. I pictured the half-empty bottle of Beefeater in the kitchen, but the idea of getting drunk had no appeal.

I couldn't read, and I knew I couldn't sleep, but I had to do something to occupy my mind. At last, I seized on Marian's murder. Puzzling over it had distracted my mind the night before my father's funeral, and it remained an intriguing puzzle, with even more loose ends now than then; trying to bring some order to it could keep my mind busy if anything could.

I didn't for a moment think that anything would come of it. It was just a way of avoiding dwelling on my father's letter and the things it made me realize about the two of us. At first I had trouble keeping my mind on the task, but in time I got control of myself and the pieces began to fall together one by one. With startling quickness, it all began to make sense. From total confusion, a pattern began to emerge, hazy and indistinct at first, but clearing rapidly until at last I understood it all. All, that is, except for two small points.

I looked at my watch. It was twenty past ten. I marvelled that it was no later, then I picked up the phone and called the police station.

The desk sergeant told me that Ben was out on a call but would be in later. I left a message for him to phone when he got in.

I had intended to give everything to Ben and let him handle it from there, but that was impossible. I still didn't want to think about anything but the James-Tyrell case, and those two pieces of the puzzle were still missing, so I picked up the phone again and dialed Harrison's number.

He answered after the second ring.

"Harrison? This is John Forest. How are you feeling?"

"Better, John. Thank you."

"You think you could stand some company for a few minutes?"

"Tonight? I was just getting ready for bed. I haven't been resting well since—" There was a long pause, then he repeated, "I was just getting ready for bed."

"I won't keep you long, Harrison. I just want to ask you a couple of questions."

"All right, John," he said after a moment's silence. "I'll turn the front porch light on for you."

"Thanks, Harrison. I'll be right over."

I hung up the phone, took a moment to arrange my mind, and then walked out the door.

Harrison's house was not far from my apartment, and I walked the distance in a few minutes. The night was cool, but a light sweat filmed my forehead as I turned on to High Street and saw the Tyrell house ahead on my right. The porch light gave the illusion of flickering rapidly on and off as the many trees which dotted the property occluded the light from my eyes.

Harrison opened the door as I climbed the steps. As I crossed the broad porch, I noticed that he was still dressed in a shirt and slacks, though he did have slippers on his feet.

"Come on into my study," he said after we'd exchanged greetings, and I followed him into a large room filled with books and theatrical memorabilia.

When I was settled into a comfortable armchair, he gestured toward a cabinet filled with an exotic assortment of bottles and asked, "Will you have a drink?"

"Thanks, Harrison," I said, getting up and walking over to the cabinet. Some of the bottles were unopened, their seals still intact. I indicated one of them. "Some Irish Mist, please."

He opened the bottle, splashed a little into a small snifter, and handed it to me. I took it back to my chair as he poured a drink for himself. I glanced around the room, looking at the framed playbills that hung on the few stretches of wall that weren't covered with bookshelves or display cases. Despite my ignorance of matters theatrical, I recognized a few of the actors—Gillette, Gielgud, Olivier.

I turned back as Harrison settled himself into a comfortable chair a few feet from the one I was in and placed a glass half filled with amber fluid on the small table which sat in the angle between our chairs.

"It's a lovely room, Harrison," I said.

He smiled as he replied, "Yes, isn't it. With Marian gone, just about everything I care about is within these four walls."

I looked at him for a long moment without speaking, and the smile went out of his eyes. But his lips were still smiling as he spoke: "What were the questions you wanted to ask, John?"

I did not speak immediately. I held the glass beneath my nose and inhaled the aroma before I took a sip. He hadn't given me very much, not even half of what he had poured for himself. I sipped at it appreciatively.

"Actually, Harrison, I think I already know the answer to one of the questions, but I'd like for you to confirm it. Why did you murder your wife?"

His hand, which was bringing his glass to his lips, stopped abruptly halfway to its destination, and several drops of liquor slopped over the rim. He appeared not to notice.

"What are you asking?" he barked out in apparently honest consternation.

I shook my head slightly in sincere admiration. "You really are good, Harrison. You would have made a wonderful actor. You should have chosen that career, you know. If you had, none of this would have happened."

"What on earth are you talking about, John? You don't really think I killed Marian. You couldn't think that!"

"But I do, Harrison. I really do." I took another sip of the Irish Mist. So little remained that I had to tip the stem high in the air to get enough to taste.

"Here," he said, extending his hand and starting to rise. "Let me get you some more."

I waved him back. "No, Harrison. Don't trouble yourself. I know where the bottle is." The truth was, I didn't trust him to refill my glass now that he knew I suspected him. I had taken the drink from him when I arrived because he didn't know what I was there for and because I could see that the seal on the bottle had not been broken. Now, however, I was taking no chances. I went to the cabinet and poured a large dollop into the snifter, then I took it back to my chair.

"I know you did it, Harrison, but I wish you'd tell me why."

Harrison was the very picture of a wronged and misunderstood man. He spread his hands helplessly before him and appeared to be on the verge of tears as he spoke: "But I loved her, John. I had no reason to kill her."

"Maybe you loved her. I'm not sure enough about what love is to say that you didn't." Images of my father's and Corinne's faces floated before my mind's eye for a moment. "But, love her or not, you did kill her. Why?"

"Why can't I make you understand? I couldn't kill her. I couldn't kill her because I loved her, and I couldn't kill her because it was physically impossible for me to have done so. She was dead when I got home. I saw her murderer disappear into the back yard from her bedroom window. And I couldn't have killed Dighton. The police know that Marian and Dighton were murdered by the same person, and I was in Washington the night he died."

He was utterly convincing, and all of a sudden I was uncertain. Not that he had done it, but that he would ever be found guilty by a jury. The man was absolutely brilliant. I took a large sip from the snifter and held it in my mouth for a long moment before swallowing.

"You were the killer who fled into the night, Harrison. Only you came back. Then you waited for the police and told them what you wanted them to believe."

"This is nonsense, John." His voice was now firm and cold. The bereaved husband role was put aside in favor of one whose principal component was righteous indignation. "You'll find yourself on the receiving end of a slander suit if you don't watch it."

"There's no one here but the two of us, Harrison. Besides, I'm just saying what we both know to be true."

He stared at me frigidly. "Suppose you tell me what it is that we both know to be true," he said.

I felt a bit uncomfortable, and I took another sip of my drink to cover my hesitation as I thought. I didn't believe that I was in any danger. I had considered the risks before I came over, but they had seemed acceptable when the alternative was staying alone in my apartment with my thoughts. There was only one way that I was any good to Harrison as a corpse, and that was dead in my bed, smothered by a pillow, and I wasn't anywhere near my bed at the moment. I was sure he wouldn't shoot me or knife me or bludgeon me to death; that would give the police an inconsistency to follow up on, and murders of that sort invariably leave clues. I might bleed on his carpet, for example.

Besides, what I knew about him, even when I passed it all on to the police, might not be enough to convict him. It might and probably would convince the police, but cops and juries are two different things. He might well get off if tried for his wife's murder alone, but if he killed me he would just be tying the noose around his own neck. Unless, of course, he could arrange to smother me to death in my own bed with my own pillow, and I didn't think there was much chance of him managing that.

From the look in his eye at that moment, I was sure that if my bed and pillow had been handy he would have made a try for it right then. But they weren't, and he knew that he could only hurt his case by dealing with me in any other fashion. So I still didn't think I was in any danger, but my discomfort remained.

"All right," I said at last. "I'll tell you what I know, Harrison. It can't hurt anything; you already know it, too. And then maybe you'll tell me if I'm right about why you did it. That's why I came tonight, Harrison: my damnable curiosity." That wasn't the whole reason, but I wasn't going to explain that to him.

"Go on," he said. The cold hostility in his voice was not an actor's trick. Convincing though he had been in his earlier roles, there was no question but that the real Harrison James, full of frustration and rage, was sitting scarcely an arm's reach away from me.

I opened my mouth to speak and was surprised to find that it was dry. I took a sip from the snifter then tried again.

"It started quite by accident, I suppose. Not your murder of Marian; that was deliberate. I mean the way you did it. Your flight back from Washington a few weeks ago got in at two-thirty, nearly half an hour after the afternoon papers were put on the stands. Did you buy a paper at the airport? Probably you did, and you read it in the cab on your way home. In it you found a short article on an inside page which related how one John Dighton, an eighty-three-year-old retired postman, had suffocated to death in his bedclothes the night before.

"The name John Dighton was what did it, wasn't it, Harrison?" I paused, but he gave no indication that he intended to answer. It was clear, however, that I had his attention. "You must have been thinking about murdering Marian for some time before that, but when you saw that a man named John Dighton had died in that peculiar fashion, it must have seemed an omen to you, who had the starring role in Shakespeare's *Richard III* not long ago. And it was at that moment, riding home from the airport in that cab, that you decided how you would kill your wife and draw suspicion away from yourself."

Harrison broke his silence. "You at least acknowledge that I did not kill Dighton, then?"

"Of course, Harrison. Nobody killed Dighton. He was just an old man who died accidentally in his sleep. But from the sketchy details in the newspaper you thought that it might be possible to make people believe that he had been murdered. If you succeeded at that, and at linking Dighton's 'murder'—for

178

which you had a perfect alibi—with the murder of your wife, you would be in the clear."

I took another sip of the Irish Mist. It didn't taste as exquisite as earlier; it seemed slightly bitter. Maybe I was getting a cold.

"After you got home from the airport, you wrote the first notes—one for the newspaper and one for the police—on ordinary writing paper and then you dropped them in the mail, after first making certain that you had left no fingerprints to link them to you."

"This is all fascinating, John," Harrison sneered. "But how did I manage to mail another pair of notes after Marian's death, when I was in police custody continuously from the time I found her dead until they released me late the following afternoon? The police arrived here a mere eleven minutes after I left the rehearsal. Are you suggesting that I drove home, a distance of eight blocks, went down to the basement and broke out a window, set up a complicated scenario in Marian's bedroom to make it appear that she had been killed by someone else, murdered her, sat down and wrote two notes, strolled out to a mailbox to post them, came back in and telephoned the police, and was waiting for them when they arrived, all in the space of eleven minutes? Bah! It isn't humanly possible."

I nodded. "You're right, Harrison. The way you tell it, it's not possible. But that's not the way it happened. You broke out the downstairs window when you were home for lunch. It rained Tuesday morning, but there was no evidence that it had rained in the basement, so the window had to have been sound until nearly noon when the rain stopped. And you were constantly in somebody's company from the time you returned from lunch until you left the rehearsal. So you had to have broken it then. As for the notes, you could have written them at any time and carried them around with you until an opportunity to use them presented itself. As it happened, I suspect that everything went according to plan, that this was the first chance you had and you took it.

"You left the rehearsal at 11:54 and drove straight home. There was no traffic at that hour of night, and you could have made it in four or five minutes, easy, driving within the speed limit and stopping at all the stop signs. Had you run into any delays you could have postponed your murder until another night. You went straight up to Marian's room and found her asleep. She woke up when you put the pillow over her face, but her arms were pinned beneath the covers and all she could do was struggle feebly until she lost consciousness. You had to hurry, but you also had to make sure that she was dead, so you probably kept the pillow over her face for several moments after she stopped struggling, then you checked her pulse to make sure that her heart had stopped as well."

I was dry again, so I drained the last of my drink before continuing.

"Then came the riskiest and the boldest part of your plan. Once you were sure Marian was dead, you deliberately knocked over the table beside the bed and raised the window as far as it would go. You then climbed out on the roof, dropped to the patio, and sprinted across the back lawn to a weak spot in the hedges. The police could tell that someone had used that opening to get through the hedge, but it didn't occur to them that someone had first gone out and then come back in through it, as you did. Once through, you were within a hundred yards of the mailbox at the corner of Pinnoch and Radd Streets, where all the doctors and lawyers have their offices in those nice old houses. You ran to the box and dropped in your notes.

"Then you made your call to the police. What I couldn't figure out for the longest time, Harrison, was how you could have done all this and still had time to get back and call the police at 12:03. We know that's when you called, because the police log all calls that come in, and we know that you didn't leave rehearsal until 11:54 because Steven Pollett mentioned the time just as you were leaving.

"And then I remembered that there is a phone booth within a few feet of that mailbox." I also remembered the haughty little poodle that had relieved himself so disdainfully on that very box when I used the same phone to try to call Ben the night after Marian's death, but Harrison didn't look to be in a mood for such extraneous details. "You used that phone to call the station. The police said they would get a car over right away, and you knew you only had a couple of minutes.

"But a couple of minutes was plenty of time for what you had left to do, wasn't it, Harrison? You ran the hundred yards back to the weak spot in the hedges, entered the house through the back door, and stood in the downstairs hall trying to get your breath. Altogether you had run less than two hundred yards

180

after making the call, but unless someone tumbled to your trick of using a short cut and making the call from the booth, it seemed impossible for you to have mailed the notes during the period in which they must have been mailed. Going out the front and along the street, the round trip was close to six blocks, the last one on the return trip in full view of the police who were answering your call. But you could have covered two hundred yards in two minutes at a brisk walk. By running, you could do it in under a minute—which, as it turned out, left you with a minute to catch your breath. So no, Harrison, it wasn't impossible at all.

"And the cleverest thing about it was that the police had no reason at all to think that you had run away from the house and came back. It wasn't until many hours later that the note was delivered to the police station, and by that time they had it firmly set in their minds that you had remained in the house until the first officers arrived. Even the heavy breathing brought on by your unaccustomed exertion didn't give you away. The police report said that you were visibly upset when they arrived— sobbing, in fact, though you were managing to hold back the tears. But you weren't sobbing, were you Harrison? Those sobs were actually gasps for breath."

I had been holding my empty snifter all this time, and now I reached over to put it on the table beside my chair. Unaccountably, I missed the table entirely, and the delicate glass hit the carpet with a thud but didn't break. I looked down at it in wonder, and when I looked back at Harrison again I saw a smile on his face that suddenly made me very afraid.

"Yes, John. You are quite right," he said conversationally, as he leaned out of his chair to pick up the glass, which had rolled over by his feet. "You've done very well so far. Please go on."

Something was wrong. I knew it then, but I didn't know what to do about it. All I could think of was that I would be all right so long as I kept talking. It was crazy—and the funny thing was that I knew it was crazy at the time—but I didn't know what else to do. When I tried to speak again my mouth was dry; my tongue was thick and I felt a touch of nausea. I looked at my glass, which Harrison had placed on the table beside his own.

"Chloral hydrate," Harrison said, matter-of-factly. "I acquired some of it illicitly—on the street—several weeks back, when I first decided to murder Marian. I had a very nice scheme worked out, then this fellow Dighton died and presented me with a better one."

He gave me an amused look. "You look puzzled. Don't be. When you phoned and insisted on coming over, I thought maybe you were on to me but I wasn't sure, so I got a dropper full of it ready. The drink I gave you was undoctored, but after I poured my drink I squirted the drug into the bottle before putting the cork back in."

He smiled then, and I could tell that he was enjoying explaining it to me. He continued. "I deliberately gave you only a small amount of liqueur. If your visit had proved to be an innocent one, I was prepared to keep you from drinking from the drugged bottle. But when you made it clear that you knew I killed Marian, I hoped you would have more to drink. I didn't think you'd let me get you a second drink after you'd told me why you had come, and, sure enough, you insisted on pouring it for yourself.

"But go on with your story," he said in an entirely friendly voice. "That is, if you can still talk. No? Well, I'll finish it for you, though I'm sure you've got the rest figured out just as well as what you've already told me."

He leaned back in his chair and folded his hands together in his lap. After a moment's thought, he began.

"I knew that the police would regard me as the probable killer, and in fact the success of my plan depended on them taking me into custody and keeping me there until the note arrived." He smiled at me.

"It was quite clever of you to catch on to how I mailed the notes. I thought it was a very nice touch, myself."

It was my turn to be uncommunicative, as it was all I could do to keep my head upright and listen to him talk at the same time.

"As you would no doubt be explaining to me, if you were still able to speak, the notes served a double purpose. First, they connected Marian's murder with Dighton's death, for which I had the best alibi of all: innocence. And second, they gave me an alibi for Marian's death as well. You see, John, I was perfectly aware that the police logged every call, and if Steven hadn't made a remark about the time when rehearsal broke up I was prepared to do so myself. He simply saved me the trouble. I wanted to make it appear that I would not have had time to mail the notes before the police arrived. I had to assume that the police would realize that the notes would not have been mailed before the murder took place—that is, that they would realize that I couldn't afford to do that if I were the killer. If for some reason I couldn't have killed her that night, the arrival of the notes without a corpse would have ruined the whole plan. No, I had to wait until she was dead before I mailed them, and I was sure that the police would never figure out how I managed it. You outdid them there, John.

"Where was I? Oh, yes. I played the part of grieving husband throughout the interrogation. I rather enjoyed it, if the truth be told. It was a challenging role, and I really had nothing to be afraid of. I knew that when the note came the police would let me go. If they wanted to overlook the fact that I had had no time to mail the note from the time the police arrived until the note came in the mail, then they could hardly overlook the fact that I had an alibi for the night of Dighton's death.

"Everything went according to plan. Well, not everything." He looked amused. "For a while there I thought I had been a bit too clever with the notes. I didn't expect the police to make the association with Richard III from the Dighton note alone, but I was sure they would get it when the note came after Marian's death. I'm afraid I gave them too much credit. Had they made the notes public—in fact, had the newspaper mentioned the notes in its coverage of Marian's murder—someone would have made the association and passed it on to the police. But both the police and the paper suppressed the notes, and it was a week before they picked up on the princes-in the-Tower angle."

He smiled at me. I was rapidly losing my fondness for those smiles.

"I understand that I have you to thank for bringing the princes to the attention of Lieutenant Latta. I appreciate it. Actually, though, I would have made the connection quite plain in the third note—the one I intended to mail after killing Miles Forest. But when that old sot got himself killed ahead of schedule, so to speak, he disrupted my plans."

He paused for a moment, then he said, "You asked why I killed Marian. I may as well satisfy your curiosity on that point. It's the least I can do for you under the circumstances." That smile again. "Marian wanted a divorce so that she and Glen Riddle could be married. Losing Marian didn't particularly bother me, since there hadn't been any love in our marriage for quite some time. But I have grown accustomed to my present way of life. I love this house, probably more than Marian did, and I love this room and the things in it. I love having fine cars and taking luxurious vacations. I love being rich, and you know as well as I do, John, that a man can't be rich on a professor's salary. Marian would have taken all of this away from me when she got her divorce. She would have taken this life away. In a very real sense, John, she would have taken my life from me, so I suppose you could say that I killed her in self defense.

"Well, is there anything else?" he asked brightly. "You said on the phone that you had a couple of questions. What was the other one?"

I was having great difficulty following Harrison's remarks. My face was hot and I my breath was coming in short, shallow pants. My head had fallen over to the side, but my eyes were still half open. Harrison canted his head to the side so that our eyes were on the same plane and then leaned forward to slap me lightly on the cheek. "What was the other question, John?"

My words sounded slurred, even to me, but I forced them out—"I wanted to ask if you had intended . . . to make me . . . your third victim . . . when the other Miles Forest died."

I could tell from his expression as I spoke that he was listening intently, and he understood the question, all right. In fact, it delighted him, and he burst out laughing.

"As a matter of fact, John Miles Forest, I had decided to let it end when Miles Forest got himself run over, but now that you've presented me with this wonderful opportunity, how can I pass it up?"

His cheerful laughter was the last thing I heard before the blackness closed in on me.

18

I was inside a giant's mouth. It was pitch dark. I could hear the sound of his teeth grinding. Hear it? The noise was so loud that it made my head ache. I was safely inside the teeth, I thought. So long as I didn't move, I would be safe. If only the sound didn't hurt so much.

Suddenly the noise stopped, and I rocked a little as the giant stopped moving his jaws. I must have been lying on his tongue, but it didn't feel soft. Come to think of it, it didn't feel wet, either. I tried to touch the tongue, to feel it, but I couldn't move my arms. I felt panic rising in me as I realized I couldn't move at all. *Dear God*, I thought, *there must be something in his saliva which has paralyzed me!* For some reason, the thought of being paralyzed was more terrifying than that of being inside a giant's mouth.

All of a sudden the giant's mouth flew open, and I thought in an instant that if I could only move I could jump out and get away. But I couldn't move at all. My eyes were open, and I saw another figure outside the giant's mouth. *Jesus*, I thought, *he's going to eat Harrison, too!*

Then Harrison reached into the trunk of the car and grabbed my arm to pull me out. It all came back in an instant—the drugged drink, Harrison's acknowledgement that he had murdered Marian, and, most jarring of all, his assertion that he had not intended to kill me until I had given him a chance he just couldn't pass up.

I closed my eyes quickly so that he wouldn't know that I was conscious, if still immobile, as he maneuvered my body out of the trunk. He was in no worse shape than most American men in their thirties, but in no better, either, and it was quite a task for him to get my 180 pounds over one shoulder. I opened my eyes then and realized where we were. The noise I had taken to be the grinding of teeth had been made by the tires of Marian's Mercedes rolling over the gravel behind the building next to Palmer's Funeral Home. The small, gravelled parking lot was separated from the paved lot behind the funeral home by a five-foot-high brick wall which ran straight back from the rear of the building to a garage for hearses and limos. The back door of the funeral home, which opened onto the stairway providing rear access to my apartment, was just over the wall from where Harrison had parked the car. He grunted as he placed my limp body across the wall. He stood beside me for a while, as though debating whether to climb over the wall himself, then walked rapidly toward the alley, to round the garage and come back on the other side.

When the sound of his footsteps became faint as he moved behind the garage, I tried again to move my limbs. I succeeded slightly, but only with great effort. My legs felt especially weak. Harrison had evidently miscalculated the potency of the Mickey he had given me; I shouldn't have been conscious at all. When I heard his steps approaching on the other side of the wall I went limp again and closed my eyes, though in the darkness he probably could not have have seen whether they were open. He didn't pick me up immediately; instead, he walked up the stairs to the back door.

I heard the jingle of keys on a ring and realized that he must have taken my keys from my pocket before putting me in the trunk. He tried several before he got the right one. He grunted with satisfaction as the lock clicked back, then he pushed the door back against the wall. He disappeared for a few moments, and I could hear his footsteps mounting and then descending the inside stairs. Having confirmed that this was indeed the back way into my apartment, he came out and hoisted me onto his shoulder again.

Nearly two hundred pounds of limp human being is not an easy load, and the soft, grunting noises Harrison made as he climbed the several steps into the building showed that he was feeling the strain.

There was a light switch just beside the door, and Harrison flipped it as soon as he closed the door. A long hall ran into the building for twenty feet, to another door which always stood open, and the stairs five feet beyond. The building had been constructed some time in the last century, and the back stairs, though never intended for regular use, were spacious. The stairwell was a square shaft twenty feet on a side, and the stairs themselves were a good three feet wide. They made a full circuit of the shaft, running up two walls to the second floor landing, and then up the other two walls to the third floor. A sturdy wooden handrail prevented anyone from falling into the stairwell; another rail ran up the wall beside the stairs.

Harrison took the first flight quickly but slowed considerably on the way up to the second floor. By the time he reached the second-floor landing, where a never-used emergency door opened out of the funeral home's business offices, he was breathing so hard that he had to stand for a minute and rest, leaning against the corner.

My mind was functioning by this time, and I had no doubt whatever about what Harrison had planned for me. I had foolishly regarded myself as safe when I went to see him, because I knew he could not safely kill me except in my own bed. Now, as I hung there over his shoulder, rocking jerkily up and down as he panted for breath, I was only one floor away from that bed and the pillow that Harrison would use as a lethal weapon. Some strength was coming back in my arms and legs—how much I wasn't sure, because I couldn't test them without letting Harrison know I was conscious—but in my weakened condition he would be able to smother me to death as easily as a kitten. If he got me into my apartment, I knew there was nothing I could do to prevent him from killing me.

However, there in the stairwell I had two things in my favor. Lugging me up those stairs was taking its toll on Harrison. He was in even worse condition than I had thought and would be exhausted by the time we reached my floor. And second, he had no idea that I was conscious.

Even together, the two didn't amount to much, but they were all that I had, and if I didn't figure out some way to turn them to my advantage in the next minute or so, that minute was likely to be the last one in my life.

Harrison started to move again, laboriously climbing from step to step, pulling himself up with his free hand on the rail next to the wall. As he rounded the turn to the last flight he slowed appreciably, and I began furiously to fan the tiny spark of an idea into flame before he reached the top. There were only a few steps left when I finally worked it out.

He was carrying me feet first over his left shoulder and holding on to the wall rail with his right hand. I risked moving my head to see how far we had to go, and I saw that the support post which ran up to the ceiling was only a few feet away. One more step and I could grab it with my right arm. Harrison made one last trembling step upward, and I moved into action as rapidly as my reluctant muscles would let me. With my right hand I grasped the support post and pulled. The action torqued Harrison's upper body clockwise and brought my legs close to the wall. I bent both legs into a tuck and then kicked my right leg into the wall with all the strength I could muster, at the same time driving my left knee into Harrison's chest and pulling myself up hand over hand on the support post.

Muscles, when over-exerted, short circuit; they just cease to obey instructions from the brain. Harrison had taxed his system drastically by carrying me up those stairs, and I was counting on his muscles disobeying orders when he tried to hold on to me.

With my left knee and right leg working in concert, I managed to lever him over the guard rail, and his exhausted legs bent at the knee, flipping him over backwards. He gave way so quickly that the force of my kick carried my own body over the rail at the same time, and I hung there briefly by my right arm, listening to Harrison scream as he fell two stories to the floor below. Though it wasn't, really, much like a scream. It was more like air escaping from a punctured tire. The sound ended abruptly with a loud, unpleasant thump.

My concentrated burst of effort had expended what little energy I had accumulated since coming to in the trunk of the Mercedes, and I only had time to think, *At least I didn't let the bastard smother me to death*, before my grip came loose and I floated down to join him. I didn't feel a thing, and I suppose I must have lost consciousness on the way down. The funny thing was that I remember feeling distinctly satisfied as I wheeled through the air into darkness. . . .

I was lying on something soft. A bed. For a moment I couldn't remember who I was, and then something fell on my face and suddenly everything came back. I let out a horrible yell and brought my hands up with all the strength I could muster. It was Harrison, I thought in terror, finishing the job. I was scrambling out of the bed on the other side before I knew I had got it wrong again. First the giant's mouth, and now this.

"Damn it, John," Ben said only half-jokingly, "I ought to arrest you for assaulting a police officer—again." He stood there rubbing his middle. A book lay on the bed between us, its pages fanned out. I looked at it and at the tie that dangled from Ben's neck.

"All I do," he said, "is reach across the bed to get that book from the nightstand, and you let out a yell like a madman and punch me in the belly."

"Jesus!" I said, and let out a great sigh. I collapsed back into the bed. "Your tie must have brushed my face. I thought it was Harrison with a pillow."

Ben smiled grimly. "James is out of business now. Permanently. You want to tell me what happened?"

It was light outside, and the leaves of the trees beyond the hospital window were casting cheerful shadows into the room. I glanced at the clock on the nightstand: just short of ten a.m.

"Sure," I said, "but how about bringing me up to date first. How did I get here?"

"Now look, you," Ben began, "this is a police matter and *I* ask the questions—"

I raised an eyebrow at him, and he smiled sheepishly.

"Sorry, John," he said. "I didn't get to bed at all last night, and my nerves are about shot." He looked beat.

"Okay," he said with a sigh, "I'll give you a quick run down, then you fill me in so I can go home and get some sleep."

"Thanks, Ben."

"All right. I got your message when I got back to the station about eleven—I'd gone out on a shooting at the Spruce Motel out on Winchester. I tried to call but you didn't answer. I wasn't especially worried—hell, people have to go to the john, take showers, or do other things which keep them from answering the phone—but when there was no answer again at twelve I began to get concerned.

"I phoned Corinne Blakely and asked if you were there. She had just gotten in from covering some long meeting, and she said she hadn't seen you since the previous evening. I explained about your message and about there being no answer at your place. When she said she had a key to your apartment I said I would meet her there. We arrived at almost the same time, and I leaned on the doorbell for a minute or so before we let ourselves in.

"The apartment was dark and empty and undisturbed, but when I opened the door to the back stairs I noticed that the light was on. In these energy-conscious times that made me suspicious enough to look over the rail, and there you were."

"What about Harrison?" I asked. "He was dead?"

"As a doornail. We weren't too sure about your condition, so we phoned for an ambulance and brought you here. The doctor said you only had a mild concussion and there was nothing to worry about, but Corinne and I shared a vigil until about an hour ago."

He smiled at me. "She said she had a deadline to make. That girl has a real dedication to duty."

"Yeah," I said, returning his smile. Then I told him the whole story, starting with my phone call to Harrison, detailing our conversation, and ending with my fall down the stairwell.

"I was just lucky," I concluded, "that the fall didn't kill me as it did Harrison."

Ben gave a short, ironic laugh. "But the fall *didn't* kill him, John. This is going to appeal to your sense of poetic justice—the fall must have knocked him unconscious, but it didn't kill him. And he was alive even after you fell on him, though the doctor said his internal injuries were so extensive by that point that he would have died of them eventually. But that didn't kill him, John. *You* did—your body fell across his face, and you smothered him to death."

I shook my head in wonder and, remembering a passage from Thomas More's account of the murder of the princes in the Tower, muttered, " . . . at the stair-foot."

Ben nodded his head and said, "Fascinating stuff."

"What?" I asked. "Police work?"

"No," he answered with a smile. "History."

About the Author

Guy M. Townsend is the editor/ publisher of Brownstone Books and *The Mystery Fancier*. He is also a law student, and, to pay his bills, a probation officer. He holds a Ph.D. in British history from Tulane University, and lives happily, if hectically, in Madison, Indiana with his wife.

About the Publisher

Perseverance Press publishes a new line of old-fashioned mysteries. Emphasis is on the classic whodunit, with no excessive gore, exploitive sex, or gratuitous violence.

#1 *DEATH SPIRAL, Murder at the Winter Olympics* $6.95
    by Meredith Phillips (1984)

It's a cold war on ice as love and defection breed murder at the Winter Olympics. Who killed world champion skater Dima Kuznetsov, the "playboy of the Eastern world": old or new lovers, hockey right-wingers, jealous rivals, the KGB? Will skating sleuth Lesley Grey discover the murderer before she herself is hunted down?

Reviews said: "realistic" (Howard Lachtman), "fair without being easy to solve" (*Drood Review*), "very engaging" (John Ball), "strongly recommended" (BBC Radio), "timely and topical" (Allen Hubin), "appealing" (*Oakland Tribune*), "informative and entertaining" (Carol Brener), "fascinating" (*San Jose Mercury*), and "authoritative" (*San Francisco Chronicle*).

#2 *TO PROVE A VILLAIN* $6.95
    by Guy M. Townsend (1985)

TO ORDER: A check for $8.00 covers retail price and shipping for each of these quality paperbacks.

Mail to

Perseverance Press
P. O. Box 384
Menlo Park, CA 94026

California residents please add 6½% tax ($.45) per book.